Web of Lies

Priya ki Kahani

To Kusumika

Best Wishes

Rashmita 2·11·08

Web of Lies

Priya ki Kahani

Rashmita Patel

DTF Publishers & Distributors
Birmingham B21 9ST

www.rashmita.org

Published by
DTF Publishers & Distributors
117 Soho Road
Handsworth
Birmingham
B21 9ST

Email: info@dtfbooks.com
Website: www.dtfbooks.com

ISBN 1-901363-63-5
First Published 2008
© 2008, **Patel**, Rashmita

Printed in Great Britain

Acknowledgements

To my loving husband, Paresh and my beautiful son,
Vivek for all their enthusiasm, patience and
encouragement.

With warm thanks to Ultimate Proof Publishing Services,
Cheltenham, for their superb guidance and editorial skills.

To all those who have read and contributed to the
manuscript along the way.

Prologue

You know, I always thought life was so wonderful, full of joy and laughter, I suppose when you're a kid that's how life is. You've got no responsibility; it's what I call a 'chilling life'. Parents take care of all the big things while you just enjoy it. They take care of the bills, the food and everything else. I guess you don't really understand responsibility until it hits you square in the face.

To some extent I've always lived in a fantasy world. I dreamt of falling in love, having a few kids and living happily ever after. But what I forgot is that falling in love isn't as simple as ek,do,tin. You expect life to fall into place after you've met the right guy but you don't think of all the complications that come after meeting him. You never consider that your life could turn into such turmoil after meeting your dream guy, but he soon becomes the centre of your attention and everything else around you comes second.

My story is somewhat regrettable; I blame most of it on myself. Maybe I just wanted to grow up too quickly and forgot who the most important people in my life were; instead I focussed on a life of lies, which got me nowhere but in trouble as you will see.

My name's Priyanka Roy. Everyone calls me Priya for short, apart from the odd few who love calling me Priyanka. I guess I don't really mind as I like both names.

I come from a small family here in the outskirts of Birmingham, the heart of the Midlands. I was born and bred in Birmingham, and just like any other teenager who lives in 'Brum', I have the 'Brumi' accent to go with it. A lot of people say that I use a lot of Brumi slang but I love it, because it makes me feel like a typical Brumi, which I am proud to be and, just like any other British Asian Girl (B.A.G), I too wanted to enjoy my teenage life.

This story is about something that happened to me when I was just seventeen and studying Art and Design at college. You must be thinking what could possibly happen at seventeen when you're still just a kid, but I went much, much further than I should have.

I was on cloud nine; I was at college; I was 'The Priya' who went out with gorgeous Sunny Deol. OK, so maybe he wasn't *that* Sunny Deol from the Bollywood films but he was *my* Sunny. Love was very much in the air for us and for a while I forgot who I was, what I believed in and, most of all, my culture.

Sunny and I had been going out for nearly two years. I met him at college in the canteen. It was weird really because it was the last place I'd thought I would meet my ideal guy. He was sitting with a group of lads and I was sitting with a few of my friends. He kept looking at me and finally, as I was leaving, he came over and asked me to go out with him. I was astounded. What could I say? I just looked at him and said yes! He was gorgeous!

I always called him Sunny although his real name was Sundip Rai. It wasn't a name I had made up; in fact when we met at school all his mates called him Sunny, and I thought the name suited him quite well. Sunny wasn't the same religion as me, he was a Punjabi whereas I was a Hindu. It didn't matter to us what religion we both were although we knew it would matter a lot to our parents.

Sunny was the kind of lad who admired himself because he had the looks and the macho body that all the other guys dreamed of. He flirted a lot with girls but not in a bad way. Most of the girls fancied him, but no one dared say they loved him as they knew he was dating me! I liked him because he stood out from the crowd; he was quite a straightforward guy who didn't really worry about what other people thought of him.

Our relationship worked well because we shared the same interests. He liked me because I didn't back chat like most girls at college did. He said I had a good sense of humour and I was very easy to be with. He said that compared to other girls I didn't have an ego problem, he saw me as a down-to-earth girl who got on with anyone. I was one of those girls who got on better with guys than with girls; I don't know why that is but I felt that the guys talked about things which were relevant while the girls just gossiped about things they had eavesdropped about on the way to college.

Sunny's dad was quite strict but not to the extent that he couldn't do what he wanted to do. His dad wanted what all dads desired and that was for Sunny to reach the top, and he was trying very hard to make it into uni this year. His family didn't know that he was dating me. I don't know how they would have reacted if they found out. Sunny said that his dad would never consider letting me in the house as I wasn't Punjabi. I don't know why but religion still plays a big part when it comes to choosing a partner. I've never quite understood it but one day I'm going to get to the bottom of this problem, I swear!

To tell you the truth, I wasn't sure whether I had a crush on Sunny or whether I was in love with him, all I knew was that I wanted to be with him 24/7 and he made me smile. My mates all believed that it was love as I had very strong feelings for him. Each time he was near me I felt myself go all funny inside.

Sunny and I were very affectionate but our relationship wasn't based on sex but on a mutual understanding with each other. Sunny wasn't like the other lads who wanted just one thing. Of course we kissed and he flirted with me but he knew when to draw the line. However, this time we didn't draw the line and we got carried away to such an extent that the results of our actions were finally shown by a thick blue line on the stick in my hand – I was PREGNANT!

Life doesn't always turn out the way you expect it to. Living in a fantasy land isn't what life is really about, so if that's how you see life, then if I were you, I'd snap out of it right now or prepare to face the consequences. As you will see, I had to learn this the hard way.

CHAPTER 1

Priya's pregnant (0-8 weeks)

I don't really know how I got into this mess. It wasn't like it was meant to be but somewhere along the line I had made the biggest mistake I had ever made in my life, a mistake that was going to cost me heavily for the rest of my life. I hadn't told anyone yet but I knew that if I didn't get myself to wake up to reality then I was going to head for big trouble very soon.

First I kept denying it to myself. I mean how could it possibly happen to me? How could I be pregnant? But, the more I tried to deny it, the more the reality began to sink in. Had I been that stupid? What would happen when Mum found out? I just wish I could make myself disappear or something. Each evening I stayed in my bedroom thinking about what i was going to do. I looked at my figure in the long mirror that hung by the side of my bed. I didn't feel any different or look any different, but that was soon about to change. I felt all hot and sweaty thinking about it. I didn't know who would be the right person to go to for advice but I knew that Sunny should hear the news first; after all he was half responsible, even if he didn't know it yet!

I thought long and hard about how I would break the news to him. I couldn't face him just yet. I was too scared of seeing his reaction so I decided to tell him by phone. As I sat on my bed with my mobile in my hand I thought about everything that had happened over the last few weeks – from our night together until this moment, I couldn't believe how things had changed so quickly. I rang his number and waited for him to pick up. It rang for ages and then suddenly I heard his voice.

'Hi babes, how you doing?'

For a second or two I just held the phone and said nothing.

'Hello, Priya, are you there?'

I had to say something now that I had called him,

'Hi Sunny,' I said quietly.

'Hi love, how you doing? What's up?'

'I need to talk to you Sunny.'

'Hey babes what's up? I'm listening.'

I tried so hard to tell him in the simplest way possible, but the words just wouldn't come out as I wanted them to. Then, all of a sudden, I just said it.

'I'M PREGNANT SUNNY.'

There was silence for a second or two.

'What did you say, Priya?'

'I said I'm pregnant.'

'Damn it! Are you sure, Priya?'

'Of course I am!'

'How can you be so sure that you are?'

'Because I've done two pregnancy tests at home and they both came up positive.'

'Are you sure you've used them correctly, Priya?'

'Believe me, I am pregnant Sunny, besides I haven't even come on.'

There was silence again,

'Are you there Sunny, say something?'

'You have to get rid of it, Priya.'

'What do mean get rid of it! It's our baby.'

'Yeah, but you're only seventeen!'

'Why are you shouting at me, remember it takes two to tango?! I didn't get pregnant on my own, you know!'

'I know that but listen, I know what you're trying to say but think about it Priya. You're too young to have a baby and we didn't plan to have a baby right this minute did we? I know we both want kids but not now. This just isn't the right time to have a family. What happened was purely an accident. Look, we're both in our second year of doing A levels, we can't afford to mess that up, not now babes.'

'So, what do you want me to do exactly?'

'Priya, think about it, we only have one option right now and that's for you to have an abortion.'

'So, it looks like you've made up your mind, haven't you?' I spat at him, angry and hurt that he could be so cold.

'Why don't you try and understand Priya!' Sunny pleaded.

'You couldn't care less about our baby! It's pointless talking to you! You men are all the same, you jump into bed when you feel like it and leave the rest for us women to sort out!'

'Priya, listen!'

'I'm sick of your excuses, forget it!'

'It's just not fair, Priya!'

I hung up. I'd had enough of Sunny and his pathetic excuses. Tears had already started to fall from my eyes, and I just couldn't hear the rubbish he was saying anymore. My phone started to ring but I switched it off.

How could he be so cold about our baby? I know we hadn't planned it, but it was still *our* baby, our flesh and blood. I really didn't know what made me get into bed with him in the first place. Since we had been together I had never even thought about it. He didn't force me, so why did I give in so easily. Maybe we just wanted to, I don't know. I didn't think you could get pregnant that quickly not after the first time of doing it. All I knew was that I was now in deep trouble because for one, Mum didn't know that I had a boyfriend, and secondly, I was now expecting a baby and, to top it all, I was only seventeen – was this any age to have a baby? All my other mates at college were going out with guys but none of them had got pregnant. Why, of all people, did it have to happen to me? I was more than scared; I was petrified and I just didn't know how I was going to break the news to Mum. This time I had really screwed things up. I had already started throwing up without anyone knowing but how long would I be able to hide this? Sooner or later Mum was going to suss me out. I had to think fast and I desperately needed somebody to talk to, only one person came to my mind and that was my friend Anita.

Anita Sandhu lived a few doors away from me. Her mum and my mum were very good friends. We both called each other's mum 'aunty'. We went to the same primary school and we always played and hung around together. Being the same age we enjoyed each other's company. Anita had two older brothers, who I also got on well with. Although we weren't related to one another we felt like we were – we were closer than sisters. I never thought Anita would ever leave me but a few years ago her dad was promoted at work and this meant that they had to move abroad. Anita's dad decided to accept the job offer and then within a few months they all moved over to the States. I was really sad to see Anita go but we kept in touch through email and would chat on the phone whenever we could. Mum told me that I could visit Anita if I passed my A levels and I was hoping to go over the year after finishing my exams. I was quite looking forward to seeing Anita but now things were looking bleak.

As I sat down by my computer to write to her, I thought about how I was going to tell her about the pregnancy. I felt so ashamed of myself. There were always stories about young girls getting pregnant on the news but I never imagined that it would ever happen to me! I wasn't just a B.G, I was a B.A.G which made it ten times worse. What would Anita think of me when she found out? I had to tell her because if I didn't then she would be very disappointed that I had kept a big thing such as this from her. Anyway, I trusted Anita and, if anything, maybe she could steer me in the right direction. I started typing.

Hi Anita

How are you? So, exams are going well I hear? How's your mum doing after her fall? I hope she's much better. Tell her to keep exercising her legs. Oh, by the way my mum's going to phone over the weekend to see how your mum is. I'll talk to you after they've had their natter. I'm missing you loads! Do you remember Zak from over the road, the one you fancied, well, he's just landed himself in big trouble with the coppers for stealing from the Post Office? Didn't I tell you that guy looked like trouble?

Anyway college is fine at the moment, nothing much happening.

There's something else I need to tell you Anita, I know you're not going to think much of me after I tell you but… I don't even know how to say it. You're going to be shocked when I tell you because you wouldn't expect this to happen to me. I've really screwed up, big time! You know me and Sunny, well, the fact is, I'm pregnant!

I know it sounds really bad and I know I shouldn't be or shouldn't have done it but I can't really turn the clock back can I? Please don't ask me how or why but I just had to tell you. I've got to go; I'll speak to you later.
Priya

I sometimes wondered why I got into such a mess in the first place. There was only one answer I could think of and that was I never got the love I wanted from my family. Well I can't really blame my mum because she's always been here for me, but Dad, well not really. If anything, I hated him. I live with Mum now. It's not common to hear of a single-parent Asian family, but with me it was nothing new. I was only eleven when Dad walked out leaving me and Mum behind. To tell you the truth I was glad to see the back of him. He was nothing but a loser. He didn't give me or Mum anything. I never felt he loved me or cared for anything for that matter. Mum, well she just put up with his stupid behaviour and when he finally left we were both glad to have peace in the house at last.

I still remember the way Dad treated Mum. They were never happy, as far as I can remember they argued about every little thing. It was all Dad's fault, he didn't like Mum full stop. All I know from what Grandad had told me was that Dad had gone to India to marry Mum. He brought her over but later started treating her badly. Grandad used to say that Dad was quite happy when he was first married to Mum but trouble began when, before I was born, Mum suffered a miscarriage at nineteen weeks and when he found out it was a boy, Dad was really angry because he had wanted a son. He totally blamed Mum for losing the baby. Of course, it wasn't Mum's fault but that's how Dad saw it. After that he treated her really badly; he despised everything she did for him. He was never happy with her cooking, if he didn't like it then he'd walk off. There were no family meals either because Dad would eat when or what he wanted. He didn't believe in all that 'family' stuff such as sitting down together to have a meal. Mum tried so hard but just couldn't please him. We never went on holiday together; Dad just spent time with his friends, who were obviously more important to him than us.

When Mum got pregnant again, Dad was happy once more until she gave birth to me, a girl. Dad didn't want a girl. He thought girls were of no value, which is why he never really loved me. Things got even worse between them after I was born. Sometimes, I'd wonder if I hadn't been born then maybe this wouldn't have happened, I don't know. When Mum and Dad argued I would always hear Dad say to Mum that she never gave him the son that he wanted. He said nasty things like she was cursed and she was unlucky, and stuff like that.

If there's one thing I don't understand it is why Asians are so desperate to have boys. To me it seems really stupid because it makes no difference. A baby is a baby. I just think Mum and Dad's generation needs to change their old-fashioned attitudes and get the stupid idea out of their heads that a boy is of greater value than a girl. They all believe that a boy will look after them when they are old, but that's just not the case anymore, as more and more Asians are leaving their parents in old people's homes. Can't they see that the world is changing and that they need to change with it?

Anyway, Asians are finding their own partners nowadays, so I can't see why there is a reason for all this favouritism, and why shouldn't parents leave their property to a girl? Why is it that only the boy should get the property? It's not always true that the girl will inherit her husband's wealth and property. The truth is parents should give equally no matter whether it's to a son or a daughter. Grandad used to say that children are children and there should be no differentiation between them. I loved Grandad and after he passed away I felt that the happiness and family ties that we had just vanished. He was so nice; he was the only relative I really got on with. I really miss him now that he's gone.

Things went downhill with Mum and Dad when Dad lost his job, after that he was down the pub on a regular basis. He'd come home late at night, very drunk. It was a nightmare. That wasn't all. He started hitting out at Mum for no reason. First he cut her lip, and then gave her a black eye and, on one occasion, he hit her so badly that she collapsed. Mum never called the police; I think she was so scared of him that she just kept quiet. I was petrified of him too, in case he turned on me. But then one day Mum did call the police when Dad started hitting her. It was only when he was taken down to the police station to calm down that he backed off. A few days later he packed his bags and left. We heard rumours that he was involved with someone else. I don't know whether it's true but after that we never saw him again. To tell you the truth I don't really care.

When Dad left, Gran came to stay with us. Gran was Mum's mum. Up till then Gran had lived with Uncle Nilesh but last year Uncle Nilesh passed away after having a heart attack. Mum had another younger brother who lived in India, my Uncle Mahesh, but Gran didn't really want to move back to India as she'd lived here for such a long time. As well as her brothers, my Mum has two elder sisters, my Aunty Tanuja who lives in London and my Aunty Neelam who lives just a few doors away from us. Aunty Neelam had two sons, Sahil and Karim. At first Gran moved in with Aunty Neelam but she soon fell out with her husband after she started setting her own rules within the house, which my uncle wasn't too happy about. Aunty Neelam spoke to Mum when things started to get out of hand and asked if Gran could stay with us because they were constantly arguing all the time. Mum couldn't really say no to Aunty Neelam as we had space for her to stay, although I wasn't very happy as I didn't see eye to eye with Gran either. My Grandad was really nice but Gran was a bit of a stirrer. I knew that once she'd come to stay with us she would be keeping an eye on everything I did.

Gran could be nice when she wanted to but she had a bad habit of choosing who she liked and who she didn't.

Mum said I should try and make peace with her but I just couldn't. From a young age I saw how much Gran loved her two daughters Tanuja and Neelam but she didn't have that same affection for my Mum. If she bought saris or anything for that matter, then you could guarantee Mum never got first choice. Mum seemed to lose out in everything. I don't know whether it was because she was the youngest, but I think the real reason was because both my aunties were quite well off. Well, Gran loved her possessions, everything revolved around money. She expected expensive gifts and maybe Mum just couldn't satisfy her in that way. I was sick of Mum being treated so badly by her family. It wasn't fair at all. Grandad wasn't like that. Mum got on well with Grandad but it was Gran who was the possessive one. My aunties were both in good jobs whereas Mum just worked in a small office. I never felt comfortable going to Aunt Tanuja's house. She was always bragging; we just could not fit in with them. Gran wasn't very happy when she found out that she was coming to stay with us. You should have seen her; she made such a fuss about leaving Aunt Neelam's house. I just couldn't believe she was going to come and stay with us now.

Aunt Neelam and Mum were the closest of the three sisters. If there were problems then they would sort it out between them. I really liked Aunt Neelam, particularly as she supported Mum so much after Dad left. Even though she was well off she was more down to earth than Aunt Tanuja, who I thought was a right snob. Sahil and Karim, my cousins were also quite decent. They were both older than me, but they both had a good sense of humour. Sometimes I used to go to the cinema with them or go bowling. We always had a right laugh. They didn't act like cousins in the sense that they never tried to tell me what to do; they never questioned me, which is what I liked most about them.

CHAPTER 3

It had been a few days since I had checked my emails; I knew Anita must have mailed me by now. I'd been putting it off but finally I sat down at my PC and logged on. I had received five messages, four were junk and the fifth was from Anita. I took a deep breath and double-clicked it.

Dear Priya

I'm still awake. Got exams tomorrow and I'm busy studying. I can't believe it Priya! You pregnant! Crikey what's your mum going to say to that? Talk about giving me a shock! Tell your mum before things get out of hand. I know she's going to spew but you have to.

I just can't believe it! What's going to happen with your studies and that? Are you going to quit college or what? Man, I just don't know what to say. I don't know anybody who's had a baby at your age. You must be scared Priya. Have you been to the doctors and that to get it checked? How many weeks pregnant are you? What does Sunny say about all this? I can't

believe you will be having a baby in nine months time.
I've got to go; my stupid brother's just walked in....I'll
email you again later.
Yrs Anita

That night I hardly slept. I thought about what Anita had written in her email. I kept tossing from side to side; thousands of questions were going around in my head. I put my hand on my stomach. It was a scary feeling that there was a baby growing inside me. The easy option was just to have an abortion and get on with life. I wasn't sure what I wanted. Part of me desperately wanted to go to uni but yet I didn't want to get rid of the baby. I knew I could only make one choice. My heart was telling me to keep the baby. A part of me now felt as though I had something to look forward to, something which was my own, a feeling, which I couldn't really explain.

After talking to Sunny on the phone I knew it would be hard to change his mind about the baby. He had made it quite clear that he didn't want a baby right now; I was really angry and disappointed with him. I couldn't believe that he hadn't even thought a little about keeping the baby. I knew I was all alone in this mess. Anita was right, I needed to tell Mum that I was expecting, before she worked it out herself or found out from someone else. Just then, my mobile started to ring. I looked at the screen; it was Sunny. I wasn't really in the mood to talk to him but I answered it anyway.

'Hi babes, how you doing?'

'How do you think?'

'Look, I'm sorry Priya, I know I was out of line, but it just wasn't what I was expecting to hear. You know, I was just shocked.'

'It's OK Sunny, really it's OK.'

'So, have you decided what you're going to do then?'

'No, not really. But I really don't think I should have an abortion.'

'Priya, you're only seventeen and besides how are we going to support a baby when neither of us has a job or a house or anything of our own. It's a bit crazy don't you think?'

'A lot of girls have babies and they seem to manage.'

'Well do you know any Asian girls who've kept a baby, because I don't? Come on Priya, talk real. Do you really think our parents are going to support us?'

'How do you know how it feels, after all, the baby's growing inside me not you, and how do you know how I feel right now?'

'Look, I know you're upset but Priya, think about it, abortion is the only way out for both of us. We can't do uni and look after a baby.'

'Well, we can forget uni, get jobs and look after the baby can't we?'

There was silence for a few minutes,

'Priya, you know how I feel about uni.'

'Is that all you can think of uni, uni, uni!' I shouted. 'Just try and think for a second about what I'm going through Sunny!'

There was silence and then Sunny said sadly,

'Look I'll see you tomorrow at college and we'll talk then, I've got to go now, I love you.'

Then he put the phone down. I sat on the bed and cried. I didn't want the baby growing up without a dad; I knew exactly what that was like. Up to now Sunny had been a great listener and really caring. I thought he knew how much this baby would mean to me but obviously not; when it came to the crunch he just couldn't keep to his word.

The next day my college friend, Rina, came to call for me as she usually did. I felt really tired and washed out. I had bags under my eyes and although I tried covering it up with lots of makeup it still didn't look any better. Rina noticed that I hadn't slept. It was obvious because I kept yawning all the way to college. She was going on about some assignment which had to be in that day, all I could think about was the baby. I was just nodding and saying yes to her but I was in my own little world.

On the way to college I decided to tell Rina about my big secret. I needed a friend right now, and although I had told Anita I needed to tell someone who was here with me now. Anita was too far away to offer much help. Rina was my closest friend since Anita left and, like me, she was also doing her A Levels. I trusted her and I knew that she wouldn't tell anyone.

Rina didn't mix too much with the other girls at college. If anything she was always sitting in the library with her head down in books. She wasn't into guys and all that stuff. I'm not quite sure how she did it but she only focussed on her studies. Her mind was just geared towards her career goal and that was to become an accountant, like her parents. She talked to me, but you would never see her partying or staying out late, she was a person who just got on with her own business. Rina was originally from India; her parents came to the UK when she was five years old. She was really bright and she always came first in class whenever we took exams or gave in an assignment. Her mum and dad were very strict with her though; she said it was good that they were strict because otherwise she could easily get onto the wrong path.

As we walked to college, I knew this was a good time to tell her that I was pregnant. I knew once I got to college then all my other mates would be around and I wouldn't get the opportunity to tell her. I didn't know how I should tell her but as I walked with her I just blurted it out,

'Rina I'm…pregnant.'

Rina stopped walking and looked directly at me in horror, her mouth wide open. I could see from her expression that she wasn't at all impressed with me. She stood still and then all of a sudden she started shouting at me.

'You're pregnant! Of all people you! Do you realise what you've got yourself into? How stupid of you Priya. How could you?'

'What do you mean how could I? It wasn't as though I planned to have a baby. I didn't do it on purpose, it just happened! I shouted back.

'You're not even married Priya. How could you think about having sex before getting married? You know your mum's going to kill you when she finds out. How could you be so careless?'

Rina was so mad with me that she carried on shouting at me as she walked. But everything she said was absolutely true. Suddenly my eyes filled with tears and then Rina stopped. I knew deep down that she was right but it was too late. There was no way I could turn the clock back. I had done it, and that was it. Rina knew that I was dating Sunny. She wasn't very happy about that either because Sunny was a Punjabi and I wasn't. She said it wasn't right that I was going out with someone who wasn't the same religion as me. I could never debate with her on that subject; she had such strong views. Maybe because she was originally from India, I don't know. I was born and bred here so I looked at it differently.

She always believed that there was a right time for everything to happen. I was more the opposite to her because I wanted to have fun and excitement not lead a boring life, studying all the time. As they say, you're only young once and I wanted to enjoy life to the max, which meant going out and dating. Of course studying was important to me but not to the extreme where I didn't have a social life.

'Sorry Priya,' said Rina as she saw tears rolling down my cheeks. 'Here take this,' she handed me a tissue from her bag.

'Are you OK?'

Suddenly Rina had become caring again. As we walked to college I told her all about how I got pregnant.

'Remember when I went to the Isle of Wight with Sunny and his mates and a few girls from college.'

'Oh yeah, I remember you telling me.'

'Well, while everyone went to the beach, Sunny and I got together. Sunny took me alone to this room. I thought we would just have a bit of fun together sitting cuddling or something. It wasn't often we'd have any privacy let alone our own room. Whilst we were in the room Sunny started messing around with me and I started throwing pillows at him. Then I picked up this cup of water and I threw it over him playfully. He got his revenge on me and did the same to me, but he had really drenched me. I went to dry my clothes but he wouldn't let me and then one thing led to another. The next minute we were in bed....'

'So didn't you use any protection?'

'Well I didn't have any. I told him that we shouldn't but you know Sunny, and besides, how did I know anything would happen on the first time of us doing it?'

'Oh come on Priya, we were always told when we were at school that you should always use some sort of protection or learn to say no. Didn't you think that you might get pregnant? Didn't it occur to you that what you were doing was wrong?'

'It did but...' then there was more tears, 'I couldn't help it, I didn't want Sunny to think....'

'I just can't understand how you could get carried away so easily. So, how pregnant are you?'

I looked at Rina, puzzled.

'I think about four or five weeks, how do I know, it's not as if I've had a kid before.'

'So, what are you going to do? Are you going to keep the baby or what?'

'I don't really know Rina. Sunny wants me to get rid of it....'

'And what do you want?'

'I'm not too sure; I don't even know what's right and what's wrong anymore. Anita says I should keep the baby.'

'It's got to be your decision, not anyone else's. How did you get into such a mess, I don't know?'

'I don't know if I can take on all that responsibility, a baby and that... I haven't a job or anything yet. I'm in my final year at college and I really wanted to go into Art and Design. I've really messed up. You know Rina, I'm really scared. What am I going to do?'

'You will have to make that decision Priya. I can't help you make that decision. If I was you I'd talk to Sunny and between you I'm sure you'll come up with some sort of agreement about what to do. Does your mum know?'

'Of course not, she'll hit the roof if she finds out. Never mind the baby she doesn't even know I've got a boyfriend and, to make matters worse, Gran's staying with us now, if anything she'll make my life hell, I know that for sure.'

'Oh, look Priya, there's Sunny over there with his mates,' said Rina pointing to the college gates.

'I'd better go, Rina; I'll catch up with you later. Thanks for the chat, and I'll see you in Maths, OK?'

'Alright, take care.'

Sunny was walking down the path with his mates. I wasn't sure what I was going to say to him. Rina was right, I needed to talk to him and come to a decision about what we both needed to do now. I started walking towards him. He saw me and came running.

'Hi Priya,' he said smiling.

'Hi.'

'How you been babes, are you OK?'

'Not really, I still haven't decided about, you know.'

'Listen to me Priya. I know you think you should keep the baby but think about how we're going to bring up a baby when neither of us has a job. Anyway are you prepared to have a baby right now?'

I looked at him.

'I know you're angry, but uni means a great deal to me. I've worked so hard this year. You know I messed up last year. This is my last chance darling. You know my Dad's not going to give me another chance. I have to get in, no matter what. You know Dad's been on my case ever since last year, he keeps reminding me that I have to do well otherwise he's going to get me a job at my uncle's takeaway. You know that's not what I want to do?'

'So, you've made your mind up and you want me to go with it, is that it?'

'I didn't say that, but it makes sense to have an abortion, after all we're not married or anything. Worst is that neither of our parents know about us, how do you think they're going to react if they found out that we were going to have a baby? I spoke to Matt last night and he thinks you should just have an abortion.'

'What! You told Matt that I'm pregnant!'

'Calm down babes. Yeah I told him. I needed to speak to someone you know. Are you saying that you haven't told anyone?'

'Matt won't keep his mouth shut, he'll go and blab to all his mates, and soon everyone at college will know that I'm pregnant.'

'Relax babes, you're jumping the gun a bit don't you think? Look, he's promised me that he'll keep quiet and right now we should be more concerned about what we're going to do don't you think? Oh, here comes Alex and Ranjit. I've got to go now, but I'll talk to you later, take care, love.'

He pecked me on the cheek. I nodded and walked off to my lesson.

When I got to my Maths lesson I saw Sunita, Kez, Rina and Lucy standing outside the classroom. They were all talking about this new guy who had just started college. I stood listening; my stomach was feeling a bit funny, our teacher arrived and we all walked in as she opened the door. I sat in the lesson clenching my stomach as I felt this pain coming and going. My stomach had been feeling really unsettled since I got up. I didn't know how long I was going to last sitting in one place trying to keep still. Rina kept asking me if I was OK but halfway through the lesson my tummy started to rupture inside and I desperately needed the loo. I rushed out quickly putting my hand by my mouth. As soon as I reached the toilets I threw up. Rina and Kez came running to see if I was OK. I was feeling so sick inside that I could hardly speak.

'Are you OK Priya?' Rina asked, looking really worried.

'Shall we call a teacher?' asked Kez.

'No, I'll be OK; I just haven't been feeling too good this morning.'

'You shouldn't have come in,' said Rina.
Luckily no questions were asked but Rina looked quite worried as she took me to the medical room.

'You have to go to the doctors, Priya and get some help,' she whispered to me.

'I will Rina, just give me some time.'

I sat in the medical room for a bit but I felt so bad that after an hour I decided to head home and rest.

CHAPTER 4

When I reached home, Mum was in the kitchen cooking. I could smell the boiled rice and the daal as I opened the front door. I didn't know what I was going to tell her. She was surely going to ask why I had come home early. I knew Gran would be in the house too, so for the time being I had to lie. I didn't want Gran knowing anything about me. I put the key in the front door and opened it slowly, but the stupid thing creaked loudly as it opened.

'Great! Talk about being discrete.' I muttered under my breath.

'Priya? Is that you?' She shouted as she heard me open the door with my key.

'Yes Mum,' I said quietly.

'Why are you already back from college?'

I took my coat off and went into the kitchen.

'I'm not feeling too good.'

I went to the sink and poured myself a glass of water and drank it all in one go.

'What's the matter beti?'

'I feel really sick inside, it must be something I ate.'

'Shall I make you an appointment to see the doctor?'

'No, no,' I said quickly, 'I'll be fine, I just need to rest.'

'OK, just go and lie down for a bit. I'll just finish making the daal and I'll come up to see you.'

As I walked out of the kitchen Gran was standing by the door listening to everything I was saying.

'Are you OK, Priya?' she asked.

'Yes, just got a bad stomach.'

As I lay down on the bed, I felt a bit better. I switched on the small TV in my room. I quickly got out of my jeans and t-shirt and put something a bit warmer on. The room was freezing cold. Just then Mum came up with some water.

'Here, drink some water, you'll feel better.'

I sat up and drank and then lay back down.

'Can you put the radiator on, I'm freezing?'

'Yes, when I go downstairs again. You sure you don't want me to call the doctor?'

'Yes Mum, I'm sure. If I get worse I'll tell you.'

I was feeling a bit scared inside. The last thing I wanted was the doctor coming round and telling Mum I was pregnant.

'Here, take these tablets; they'll help calm your stomach down.'

'I'll have them later Mum, my stomach has just settled down. I don't want it to explode again. Don't worry, I'll be fine. I just need to rest OK. If I feel really bad then I'll go to the doctors myself. There's a lot of this going around at college Mum. Don't worry, I'll be OK.'

'Well, call me if you need anything dear.'

'Yes, Mum, thanks.'

After Mum left, I couldn't help thinking about everything that was happening to me. The same question kept popping up in my head, what am I going to do? I still couldn't believe it, that I was pregnant. I kept convincing myself that it wasn't true but the more I thought about it the more the truth was showing. I cried silently. Was this any age to be pregnant? What was the rush? It was temptation and to show Sunny that I loved him. What else could it be? I needed to see a doctor or nurse as soon as possible. Since I had found out that I was pregnant I hadn't been to have a check up. I knew that I needed to go. I just didn't know how I was going to keep it a secret from everyone. What if someone I knew saw me at the doctors?

I had already hidden so much from Mum, the undercover mobile, the undercover boyfriend, and now the undercover baby. I felt lying to her was becoming a bad habit. I was sick of lying, I just wanted to tell Mum the truth but every time I thought about telling her, Gran would come into the picture.

I had picked up a pregnancy book from the local library on the way home. I took it out of my bag and looked at it. I felt like this shouldn't be me holding the book but someone much older. I opened it and saw lots of pictures of the baby in a mother's womb. I started to read about the baby's development. I was shocked, the baby was growing rapidly. I guessed that I was roughly about six weeks pregnant. The picture at seven weeks showed how the baby's elbow had developed and how the teeth and brain were developing. I was scared. There was a real baby growing inside me, it was alive. How could I kill an innocent life? I didn't want to. I mean, I never believed in abortion but now I was thinking about it because it was me who was pregnant. When I was at school, I remember the Religious Studies teacher asked us to debate about whether abortion was right or wrong and I still recall how much I fought in that debate to get the message across that abortion was the wrong thing to do. Now here I was pregnant myself, and considering it.

The book mentioned that women who were pregnant or who were thinking of becoming pregnant should take folic acid tablets in the first 12 weeks of their pregnancy. I hadn't even started taking anything; I didn't even know what folic acid tablets were or why you needed to take them. Then I read on that I needed to take them to prevent defects such as Spina Bifida. I thought I'd better pay a visit to the chemist and start taking them; I didn't want anything happening to the baby. Just as I was flicking through the pages of the book, Gran walked in. I quickly hid the book under the quilt. She looked at me,

'Are you OK, Priyanka?' she asked.

'Umm yes, I'm fine, really. I'm feeling much better than before.'

'Your Mum said that you've been sick. I was just thinking what might have caused it.'

'Oh well it's nothing to worry about, a lot of students at college have got this bug, it's going around our college at the moment, I'll be fine in a few days.'

'You're sure it's nothing else like….'

'Of course not, Gran, umm, I was just about to have a little nap, if that's OK.'

She smiled and walked out. I was really scared. I thought for a second or two that she had put two and two together. But how could she without any proof?

The next day I stayed at home. Sunny phoned me a few times on my mobile. I always kept my phone on vibrate when I was home in case Mum caught me. Sunny was pestering me about whether I had made a decision. I told him I wasn't feeling up to making a decision right now. For once in my life I had never felt so scared knowing I was carrying a baby inside. I could deny it as much as I wanted but the truth was I was seventeen and pregnant. I knew that sooner or later everyone would know that I was pregnant. It wasn't as if I would be able to hide it. Soon my stomach would be sticking out, oh, of all people why me? Was I having a bad dream or what? No, this was definitely real; I was going to be a mother. What was wrong with me, I wasn't dumb, I was a bright A Level student. I couldn't see myself pushing a pram just yet, let alone changing nappies. That's not how I had planned life, especially not at seventeen. I should be thinking about my career right now not family planning. Maybe Sunny was right after all. All my plans now seemed out of focus. My dream of being an art teacher seemed unreal.

I now had to make the biggest decision of my life, which would affect me for the *rest* of my life. It didn't matter which way I went either I destroyed my career goals, which

I had dreamt of for so long, or kill the baby that I was carrying. Both were very important to me. I wanted both but I could only choose one path. Maybe I could keep the baby and become a teacher later on, but I knew deep down that I would be waiting a long time for this to happen. If I terminated the pregnancy then I would be killing an innocent baby, which I felt I had no right to do. We had created the baby in the first place so how could I destroy it. Nothing made sense. I decided to go to sleep; I knew there was no way I was going to make a decision today.

I tried falling asleep, but just couldn't. The thought of the baby was keeping me awake; it had ever since I had found out. I got out of bed and sat at my computer. I switched it on and logged onto my email. I had received two new messages. The first was just another junk letter. The second was from Anita. I opened it quickly to see what she had written.

Dear Priya,

How's things at your end? I'm getting really worried about you. What's happening? I haven't heard from you. Have you and Sunny decided what you're going to do? Mum hasn't phoned because the line has been down due to the weather. It's only been fixed today. So she'll be phoning soon. I'll talk then, take care.

Anita

Ps Exams went well.

I decided to reply back to her there and then.

Hi Anita

Sorry for the delay. I'm glad your exams went well.
I'm OK, but I haven't decided what to do. I know I
should make a decision fast and I will. Sunny's made
it clear he doesn't want me to keep the baby. I know
when Mum finds out she's going to say the same. At
the moment it looks like I'm heading towards having
an abortion. I don't believe it's the right thing to do.
I'm so confused. I'll talk to you later, got to go.
Priya

I had to make my decision about the baby very soon.
Not just to solve this problem but also because if I was
going to terminate the pregnancy it had to be done before
it was too late. I had to make a decision today. I paced
up and down the room several times thinking about
everything but I just couldn't come to a decision.

I was now throwing up more frequently and keeping
it a secret from Mum was impossible. When she heard
me a few times she insisted that I go and see a doctor. To
top it all up she booked me in for the following day. So far
Mum hadn't figured out that I was pregnant. Well she
wouldn't really; I mean she didn't know that I had a
boyfriend!

I was feeling weird inside, I had leg cramps one
minute and constipation another. I didn't feel pregnant
but really ill all the time. I decided to break the news to

her before it really got out of hand. The last thing I wanted was someone else telling her that I was expecting. I thought I'd tell her first thing in the morning but I just didn't know how I'd summon the courage to do it.

That evening Mum came to my room to see if I was feeling OK.

'How are you feeling Priya?' she asked.

'I'm OK, just tired.'

'Well, I've booked you an appointment tomorrow morning to see the doctor. I'll take you down first thing and then go to work.'

'Mum, I need to speak to you about something really important.'

Mum sat down beside me on the bed.

'Are you OK?' She asked, looking a bit worried. 'What is it?'

'I know this isn't going to sound good but please don't be angry with me, I never meant this to happen Mum.'

'Have you done something Priya?'

I didn't know how to tell her. Tears fell as I whispered, 'I'm pregnant, Mum.'

Mum's face dropped.

'What did you say?' She said, totally horrified.

'I'm pregnant, Mum'.

Before I could say anymore I felt a burn on my face as she slapped me hard.

'I trusted you Priya! You kept something as big as this from me! How could you! How did I give birth to someone like you! I am ashamed of you; you aren't my daughter! Don't call me Mum, you hear me!'

Tears rolled down my cheeks. I felt scared; my heart was racing like mad. She started shouting and screaming at me.

'I'm sorry Mum, I'm really, really sorry!'

Just then Gran appeared, she stood by the door of my bedroom.

'What's happening, why are you both shouting?' she asked, looking at both of us.

Mum got up and ran downstairs. Gran gave me this look and followed Mum downstairs. All I could hear was Mum and Gran talking about me. Mum was telling Gran that I was pregnant. She was clearly very angry with me. She was telling Gran that she didn't know how she was going to show her face to anyone. I felt really bad inside, it was all my fault, how stupid of me. I could hear Gran asking all sorts of questions like who the father of the baby was – I hated to hear them talking about me like that.

I knew I had really let Mum down. I felt ashamed of myself. I couldn't believe what one stupid mistake had done to me. It had messed everything up for me, not just for me but for Mum too. I knew that soon everyone would find out about me. This was terrible. What a disaster! I shouldn't have told Mum. I should have just listened to Sunny and terminated the pregnancy. There was nothing I could say that would make Mum feel better and things were going to get worse by the day. If anything, she didn't want to see me or speak to me, she hated me. That evening I sat in my bedroom all alone. I went over to the computer and emailed Anita.

Dear Anita

I feel so down today. Just broke the news to Mum and she's really angry with me. I can't sleep, and I haven't been downstairs since I told Mum. Gran knows too, I bet she'll go and blab it to Aunt Neelam tomorrow. I'm history tomorrow! Mum's never going to forgive me. I shouldn't have told her, Anita, it was a bad move. I should have just listened to Sunny and terminated the pregnancy. I've got to go, I can't write anymore.
Priya

I logged off and went to lie down on my bed and, after a couple of hours spent crying quietly to myself, I fell asleep.

CHAPTER 5

The next morning I woke up feeling a bit worse for wear. I wasn't sure how I was going to approach Mum and Gran. I knew deep down that Mum wouldn't forgive me easily. If anything she'd be ignoring me. Mum always gave me the silent treatment when I did something wrong, but after a day or so she would come around. This time it wasn't that simple, Mum wasn't going to give in that easily. I had to go downstairs and face the music. I had a shower and got ready more slowly than usual and made my way downstairs.

Mum was in the kitchen preparing breakfast. I went in and poured myself a mug of tea. Mum didn't make any conversation; she just stood at the worktop slowly spreading margarine onto a piece of toast. I didn't really know how to break the ice; I just sat down and started to drink my tea. Gran walked in. She looked at me and then stood by Mum. Usually Mum sat down to have her breakfast with me but it was obvious that she didn't want to today. I quickly finished my tea and walked out. Mum had booked me an appointment to see the doctor this morning; I wasn't sure what to do now. She didn't mention the doctors and I knew that there was no way she was going to drive me there or even come with me. I decided not to go and went straight to college instead.

Tears fell from my eyes as I walked to college by myself. I just didn't know how I was going to handle all this. It was getting too much for me to handle. I felt alone and frightened, who would help me? It was definite that Mum wasn't going to help me. I was all alone in this stupid dilemma, I texted Rina to tell her to meet me by the library. There were a million and one things that kept coming into my head, thoughts about the baby, thoughts about Mum, and thoughts about Sunny and college. It's less commonly heard about an Asian girl getting pregnant. I'd never heard of an Asian girl getting pregnant like this. Maybe I should just have the abortion to keep everyone happy. Sunny was right about me terminating the pregnancy. I just wish I hadn't told Mum.

I had a free period first thing so I went straight to the library to meet Rina, as I was walking towards the library Kez and Lucy came running up to me.

'So, is it true Priya?' Asked Kez excitedly.

'What's true, what are you on about?'

'You know,' said Kez looking at me with excitement.

'No, not really,' I said looking totally puzzled as to what they were on about.

'We heard that you're pregnant,' said Lucy loudly.

I suddenly turned colour as I heard them say the word 'pregnant', how on earth did they know? I hadn't told anyone so how did they find out? This was terrible; I had to think of something fast.

'Oh really, and who said that I am?'

'We heard Sunny and Matt talking about it this morning outside the Art room.'

'Well you heard wrong, maybe they were talking about someone else.'

'No, I heard Matt say it was you,' said Lucy looking directly at me.

'So is it true then?' Said Kez, I could tell she was trying hard to find out.

'Well, I'm telling you I'm not, OK!' I shouted, angry that they wouldn't let it go.

'Sorry, we just heard rumours so we just thought we'll ask you whether it's true.'

'Well you're talking a load of rubbish, and anyway you shouldn't be listening to other people's conversations.'

'What's eating you up today?' remarked Lucy.

I walked off feeling ashamed and embarrassed, as I did so I could hear Kez saying in the background,

'I bet she is.'

I phoned Sunny and told him to meet me by the library urgently.

A few minutes later he appeared.

'Hi Priya.'

'You couldn't even keep your mouth shut for one minute could you?'

'What are you on about Priya?'

'Kez and Lucy know that I'm pregnant, that's what!'

'How? I haven't told them, if that's what you're implying.'

'Well they heard you talking to Matt this morning by the Art Block stupid! That's how!'

'Oh damn it! Well just say you aren't,' replied Sunny.

'Well, that's what I said but I doubt they're going to believe me, and besides it's going to look a bit obvious that I am pregnant soon.'

'How?'

'Well I keep throwing up, stupid!'

'Oh! Well I told you to have an abortion, but you wouldn't listen, would you.'

'I've decided to, OK?'

'You what...what did you say?' said Sunny, shocked.

'I said that I'm going to have an abortion.'

There was a big smile on Sunny's face as he realised what I said.

'Oh I love you, Priya. Believe me, that'll shut everyone up.'

'I told Mum yesterday.'

'You told your mum, are you mad?'

'I can't keep lying to her Sunny. She made me an appointment to see the doctor today. I couldn't lie anymore, could I?'

'Oh no, now what, what if she wants to know who the father is?'

'There's no need for you to worry, I won't dob you in that easily.'

'You know Dad will kill me if he finds out.'

'I told you I won't mention your name, and anyway Mum and Gran are both ignoring me.'

'Come here love.'

Sunny hugged me tightly, 'I love you Priya...you know that...' he whispered into my ear.

I felt better when Sunny hugged me. At least someone cared about me. I don't know how but I had now made a decision that I was going to have an abortion. I think the decision just made itself by what was happening. Soon it would be all over, then my life could get back to normal.

When I reached home, no-one was speaking to me. Aunt Neelam had come over. I had a gut feeling that Gran must have filled her in with all the juicy gossip. I went into the living room, looking slightly worried.

'Hi Aunty.'

'Hi, Priya,' she said smiling at me. 'So you just come back from college?'

'Yeah.'

Mum and Gran walked off to the kitchen as I sat down with Aunt Neelam.

'So tell me, what I've heard from Gran, is that true Priya?'

'What's that,' I said looking at her as though I hadn't a clue what she was on about.

'She said you're pregnant.'

'So what if I am, and who told her to go and blab it out.'

'They're worried about you Priya, can't you see that?'

'Well there's no need to worry because you'll be all glad to hear that I'm having an abortion.'

'Who's the father, Priya?'

'What's with all the questions?'

'Is he Hindu?'

I looked at her, what sort of question was that?

'No, he's a Punjabi.'

'Oh Priya, what's wrong with you, if anything I thought you would know better. If he was a Hindu then I would have spoken to your mother and I would have got you married with him. You know that we don't marry someone who isn't the same religion as us.'

'What difference does it make, Aunty?'

'You youngsters have an answer for everything, you only think short term, you don't think about all the problems that occur later.'

I didn't understand what she was rabbiting on about.

'I got myself into this mess, I'm sure I can get out of this mess too.' I said calmly, trying not to get angry with her.

'I'm only trying to help you; your Mum's very upset with you. You should have at least told her that you had a boyfriend.'

'What would that do, she wouldn't let me go out with him if she knew?'

'You haven't really thought about what effect this is going to have on everybody have you?'

'I know I've made a mistake but I can't really turn the clock back now can I? Mum and Gran are ignoring me, so what good is that doing me? I can't even talk to them about my future or anything for that matter.'

'Your Mum's angry at the moment; she's had a big shock finding out that you're pregnant. She needs some space. Priya, when your Mum sends you to college she trusts you, she doesn't watch you like other parents do 24/7 does she? You shouldn't have done this to her. She deserves better. I mean first your Dad and now you.'

I didn't know what to say, I just walked off feeling guilty as hell. That evening I hardly ate again. I sat in my bedroom thinking about what Aunt Neelam had said. Just then the phone rang, Mum picked it up. It was Anita's mum. I was hoping Mum wouldn't say anything about me to her. I listened by my bedroom door but it was just a general conversation. She then shouted across to me from downstairs to let me know that Anita wanted to talk to me. I grabbed the phone as Mum put the cordless back down.

'Hi Anita.'

'Oh, hi Priya, how are you?'

'I guess I'm OK,' I sighed.

'So how's things?' asked Anita anxiously.

'Don't ask, anyway, how's your mum doing?'

'She's OK, recovering slowly.'

'So, what's happening with you and you know?'

'I've decided to have an abortion.'

'No, Priya, you can't!'

'I haven't got much choice. Everyone's on my case at the moment. Sunny doesn't want me to have the baby, Mum and Gran are totally ignoring me. I won't get anyone's support. I just have to get rid of the baby. It's the only way out. You won't believe what happened at college, Kez and Lucy heard Sunny and Matt talking about me being pregnant. I don't want the whole college knowing that I am.'

'Oh boy, you're in a right mess, aren't you?'

Tears started to fall again and I started sniffling on the phone.

'Oh don't cry Priya, it'll all be sorted soon.'

'I don't know how I got into this mess, it's all my fault. I just shouldn't have. I've got to go; I'll email you later.'

'Please don't worry, take care, bye.'

I put the phone down. It was nice talking to Anita. I really missed her. If she was here right now I knew she would help me get out of this mess.

That evening Mum called me downstairs. I didn't really know what she was going to say to me. I was really worried in case she told me to leave the house. When I went down to talk to her I quickly realised that she was still very angry with me. She gave me a big lecture but I knew this was coming sooner or later.

'Priya, I don't know who the father of the baby is and I don't care either but I want you to get rid of it. Do you hear me! There is no way you're going to stay here and bring up a baby. You're not even married, what will people say when they find out? People will be pointing their fingers at me and saying, 'her mum didn't bring her up properly'. Who's going to marry you knowing that you're pregnant? I don't want this kind of sin in the house, do you hear me!'

I stood listening, with my head down as Mum continued to shout at me.

Gran sat listening to Mum silently, but I knew that wasn't going to last for too long, and then suddenly she burst out,

'I can't believe you have no shame! Did your mum bring you up like this?' She said.

'You aren't my mum, OK!'

'Priya, don't talk to your Gran like that!'

'Well, no one told her to speak!'

'Have some respect for your elders.'

Suddenly I couldn't take any more lectures from anyone; I just got up and ran upstairs.

CHAPTER 6

Priya's pregnent
(8-12 weeks)

I had booked an appointment to see Dr Helen at the Health Care Centre but was then referred to the midwife by the doctor. I decided to go alone to see the midwife. I felt kind of strange going but I knew that it was crucial for me to see the midwife. It was my first appointment and, as I waited patiently in the waiting room to be called in, I could see a few ladies sitting with their babies. They were all miles older than me and they all seemed to look like they knew what they were doing. Suddenly my name bleeped on the screen on the top wall.

Priyanka Roy Room 12

I quickly got up and walked towards room 12. I knocked gently on the door. My heart was racing as I went inside; I wasn't sure what to expect. The midwife seemed quite friendly and nice. She asked me some general questions and then she started talking about the pregnancy. She asked for a sample of my urine, and checked my blood pressure which were both fine. She gave me a lot of forms to fill in. They were all general forms about family health and about my health generally.

She asked me questions about my boyfriend and my mum too. I knew I was terminating the pregnancy just to please everyone; it was not what I really wanted. Deep down if I had it my way I wanted to keep the baby.

I told the midwife that I was throwing up quite a lot. She looked at me.

'Priyanka, this is what we call morning sickness, and a lot of women who are pregnant get morning sickness in the first twelve weeks, it's all because of the physical changes happening inside your body and increasing oestrogen levels. You'll find after twelve weeks the sickness should start to wear off. Try eating biscuits and crackers, you'll find it does the trick for many pregnant women. Is there anything else that you are suffering from?

'Not really, just a bit constipated.'

'That's another common thing women suffer in the first trimester. Try eating more green vegetables.'

The midwife pointed out some key things that I might experience.

'You might start to crave certain foods. Not all women crave but some crave for particular foods.'

'When would I start to show?'

'Oh, you've got a while before that starts to happen, usually it's around sixteen weeks that you start to look pregnant.'

I got really stuck for answers when she started to ask me things about the father. I mean, health-wise, I didn't know much about Sunny, but I tried answering what I could. She asked when my last period was and then calculated from that my Expected Due Date. Surprisingly I was seven weeks pregnant; I couldn't believe it!

I then told her that I wasn't going to keep the baby that I wanted to have an abortion. The midwife was really nice and asked me why I felt like that. So I told her everything about my reasons for wanting to get rid of the baby. She explained to me about the cooling off period and she also talked about the option of me having the baby adopted. There was so much going on in my head about this pregnancy that it was impossible for me to think straight. The idea of having the abortion was killing me; all I could think of was that there was a real baby growing inside of me. After a long chat with the midwife she explained the procedure. She explained to me that I would have to go to the Family Planning Clinic to have the abortion carried out because they didn't do it at the Health Clinic, and that the waiting time could be anything from two to four weeks for this to happen. I was shocked as I thought they did it straight away.

'Isn't there any way I could have it done straight away?' I asked.

'Well there is, you could have it done through private care but it's quite expensive. Is there anything else you need to know, Priyanka?'

'Just one more thing,' I asked. 'How do they actually carry out the abortion because I'm really scared about this?'

'Oh don't worry, its usually done by a method called Vacuum Aspiration which is a suction method whereby they stretch the cervix and pass a tube into the womb and then remove the pregnancy by suction.'

'Will it hurt?'

'Usually it's carried out under a general or local anaesthetic. I'm not saying it's totally painless but you should only feel a bit of discomfort when they do it.'

The midwife explained all the options available to me and the risks involved. She said that she would be sending a letter to the clinic for the termination to be carried out, after that I left the Health Care Centre.

As I walked home my mind was focused only on two things, which were the baby and the abortion. Thoughts of Sunny kept coming into my head. I kept looking at my mobile wondering whether I should ring him and talk to him about my appointment. At one point I nearly rang him but the thought that he wasn't the caring Sunny I knew when I met him stopped me. Each time I talked to him I felt all he was interested in was his future and how much uni meant to him. He hadn't even thought a bit about our future. Here I was joined to the hip with him but now, for once, I felt that wasn't the case anymore. If he cared so much for me then surely he would have thought about the baby for at least a second. All he cared was that no one found out about us and the baby. It was very big of him to *act* like he was all mature and grown up but that wasn't true. He was just a coward. He only cared about what would save his dignity. Was this the guy I had fallen madly in love with? Why did I feel like his love wasn't as real as I imagined. Was Sunny really in love with me? Or was it just to show everyone that he had a girlfriend. For once I had started to look at Sunny in a very different light.

Maybe I trusted him too much, was this because I was looking for love after Dad left? After all I always did talk to Sunny about Dad. He was the only one I could really talk to. Maybe I was being selfish too. Did I really love Sunny or was I just after someone to talk too? I felt I had all these questions stuck in my head but no answers to go with them. It was like trying to put a jigsaw together where you couldn't find the pieces to fit.

When Mum found out a few days later that I had been to the doctors she was quite curious about finding out what had happened. She got Aunt Neelam to ask me indirectly whether I had the abortion. Of course I had to lie so I pretended that I had to go and have the abortion done on Friday. When Friday came I pretended to go to the Health Clinic. Aunt Neelam offered to come along but I refused as I didn't want her finding out that I was lying about the date. When I came home I went straight to my bedroom. Mum didn't question me or say anything for the matter. I think in the back of her mind she was relieved that I had terminated the pregnancy. I had lied to Sunny too, I was pretty mad with him because he never even once asked me that he would come with me when I was going to have the abortion carried out. It wasn't like I was asking for too much; all I wanted was a bit of moral support.

CHAPTER 7

Out of the blue a week later Mum received a call from India, it was Uncle Mahesh. I sat in the living room watching TV as Mum was speaking to him. I couldn't help overhearing the conversation, Uncle Mahesh was telling Mum that my cousin sister, Sneha had been fixed up. Uncle Mahesh was Mum's younger brother. I was happy to see Mum smiling again. Mum was on the phone for at least a quarter of an hour as Uncle was talking about the wedding. Meanwhile I went into the kitchen as I was craving for some vanilla ice-cream and pickle!

Then the big shock came when she asked me if I would go with her and Gran to India. I was astounded; I didn't know what to say? I hadn't been to India before but I really didn't want to go either. This was awful, for once, Mum and I were just about talking again and now another storm had hit us again. I didn't know what to say. The only excuse I had was exams and revision. Mum seemed disappointed. She really wanted me to go. I knew if I didn't go then Mum wouldn't go either, she wasn't going to leave me here on my own. Mum said that it would do me some good as I hadn't been to India before. I didn't know what to say. I couldn't go, but how could I explain that to Mum. I couldn't really tell her the reason why I didn't want to go. But, by the end of the evening Mum and Gran had literally turned my decision around to go to India. She was so persuasive that I somehow ended up saying yes. I couldn't believe it. Why did I always land myself in trouble?

Mum had phoned Aunt Neelam to see if they were going to come along, but she said that she was going to give this a miss as uncle hadn't been in good health for the last few months. Karim and Sahil said no too as neither had any holidays left from work. Mum asked Sahil to sort out the tickets for us to fly over the following week. I couldn't believe how quickly Mum organised things. Sneha's wedding was fixed for the end of the month. We really needed to fly out some time next week. I can't say I wasn't looking forward to going as I had never flown before, and I was really looking forward to that. The biggest thrill was to see India; I had always wanted to go to India but never had the opportunity. I wanted to see for myself how things looked in another country. I had heard so much about the villages, the food, and the people and wanted to experience it for myself. I had heard that shopping was the best part of it all. Mum had told me shopping in India was really exciting and that was something I was quite looking forward too.

Mum and Gran had already started to pack. Well we had to, we were going next week! Sahil had booked the tickets and everything was sorted. I decided to e-mail Anita to tell her that I was off to India for a few weeks. I didn't really want to discuss anything more than that with her because I just didn't know what to say to her.

Dear Anita

Just letting you know that I am going to India for three weeks. I haven't got time to discuss everything as I don't even know what I'm doing. I'll email you when I get back. Take care and say hello to everyone for me.
Love
Priya

When I broke the news to Sunny that I was going to India for a few weeks, he was shocked.

'Are you serious, why all of a sudden?' he asked

'My cousin sister's getting married and Mum has told me to come, so I'm going.'

'I'm going to miss you babes.'

'Me too.'

'So when are you going?' he asked.

'Next Saturday.'

'Crickey! That's a bit quick isn't it?'

'Mum's arranged everything, can't back out can I?'

'You don't seem very happy about going.'

'Well, I didn't really want to go, not right now but I've got no choice. Mum persuaded me to go. If I don't go then things between me and Mum just aren't going to get any better. I don't want to lose her.'

'Don't worry, you'll be back soon, and anyway after

all this business with the baby and the abortion you need a break.'

I looked at him,

'I presume so, oh, can you tell Rina when she gets back from London that I've gone to India; I tried ringing her on her mobile but she's not answering.'

'Yeah, don't worry, I'll tell her. Make sure you come back quick babes, I'll be waiting.'

He kissed me on the lips.

'Not here, Sunny, someone might be watching us.'

'Oh don't worry, let them talk.'

'Stop it.'

'Sometimes I just don't understand you, Priya.'

'I've got to go.'

'See you later honey.'

'Bye.'

The day had come for us to fly to India. In the morning we went to Aunt Neelam's to say goodbye, Sahil and Karim came later to take us to the airport. When we reached the airport we checked in our baggage. Luckily we didn't have any problems with the weight, which was surprising as Mum had packed enough for three months let alone three weeks!

'Hey sis, have a nice time and don't forget to bring my halva will you?' said Karim.

I hugged him and smiled.

'Of course not and what do you want me to bring you, big brother?'

Sahil looked and smiled.

'How about Raja Hindustani.'

I laughed.

'It's not me who's going to get married remember, its Sneha.'

He smiled.

'I'm just joking,' he said and gave me a big hug.

We said our farewells and went through the departure gate.

Mum kept reminding me about my malaria tablets. She was more worried than me in case I got ill over there. I kept nodding.

'Where are the passports and tickets?'

'Don't worry Mum, I've got them right here'

I hadn't been abroad before, and flying for the first time was absolutely wonderful. I was quite scared when it took off, my ears went all funny, but Mum gave me some sweets to chew on. She said that chewing helped the ears from popping – she was right as usual. It was a nine-hour flight. I was feeling better as my morning sickness had calmed down. The food was delicious and I quite enjoyed the flight. As we approached India I could see millions of tiny lights through the cabin window. It was dark outside. I was getting so excited I couldn't even sit in my seat anymore. My eyes were glued to the window. The plane kept tilting from side to side which was scary. Suddenly we were all told to fasten our seatbelts as the plane was going to land. The plane thudded as it hit the runway. I quickly held onto my seat. The plane started to jerk before it finally hit the ground. At last, we were here!

As the plane landed everyone rushed to get their belongings together. It was terrible; people were pushing and shoving each other like little kids. Mum told me to wait. I couldn't see what the rush was. When we got out, we made our way to customs and when I saw the queue I realised why everyone was rushing so much! You couldn't even see where each queue started and ended. We waited in what looked like a queue. Finally when it was our turn Mum handed the customs man our passports and tickets, he checked and stamped them. We then left customs and headed towards the luggage collection. The luggage had already started to come out on the conveyor belts. We waited and waited for our suitcases to come and then finally we spotted them. Mum was very quick; she just pulled each suitcase off one by one. I went and got a trolley and then we joined another queue to get out of the airport before leaving.

As we came out there were loads of people waiting to meet relatives. Mum spotted Uncle Mahesh who stood quite near to the entrance. We all greeted each other and then he took us to his van. It was night time when we arrived and as we approached home to a village called Dandi it was starting to get light. Mum and Uncle Mahesh chatted all the way. As we travelled from the airport to the village I looked outside, I was truly amazed. I just couldn't get over the fact that I was now in India. The weather was fantastic and I was so amazed by what I saw. The roads were similar but instead of houses there was a scatter of villages here and there. The shops weren't big they were just small individual shops. The only thing I hated was the loos. They weren't how I imagined, just a hole in the ground, not something I was used to. The best bit was that Dandi was by the sea and I knew that if I got bored I could always go down and have a nice stroll by the beach.

When we arrived at Dandi, I saw Mum's face light up. Everyone was hugging and crying. I didn't really know who was who. My aunt did a tilak on our foreheads and gave us a flower to welcome us to their home. I felt really honoured. We went inside, it was quite dark inside. The fan on the ceiling was on and it made this funny squeaky noise. Sneha who was my cousin came and sat by me. I hadn't really seen her before, only in photos. We all freshened up and had something to eat. While Mum talked to the adults, Sneha came over to talk to me. I started talking to her about her marriage. She showed me a picture of the guy she was engaged to. He was quite a good-looking guy. I was quite looking forward to the wedding I'd heard that weddings in India were miles better than weddings in Britain.

CHAPTER 8

Later that day Sneha took me outside. It was quite pleasant out in the front yard. There were a few hens walking around and a peacock. It was funny; it was just like visiting an English countryside. By late afternoon Sneha had started making dinner with her Mum. I asked if they needed a hand but they seemed to cook in a different way and I wasn't sure how I could help, I just watched as they cooked. Sneha sat on the floor making chapattis and her Mum started cooking a vegetarian meal. The first night was a bit tiring. We were all jet lagged, so after dinner we all went to sleep.

I was quite enjoying the stay because there was so much to see and do but after a few days I started feeling a bit home sick. I was missing Sunny a lot. The food here just didn't taste as good as food Mum cooked at home. As the wedding drew nearer and nearer, Uncle Mahesh was asking if Mum wanted me to find a guy here too. I thought it was all a joke at first, but the joke soon wore off as I overheard Mum and Uncle Mahesh talking seriously about my wedding too. I was really angry. At first I pretended as though I didn't know what they were on about but things got out of hand when they started phoning around and calling guys to come and see me. I was now panicking and wanted to go home desperately. Was this what Mum and Gran had in store for me? It now made sense why Mum wanted me to come over to India. She planned to get me fixed up so that people would stop gossiping about me. I just knew that Gran was up to her old tricks again. But there was no way I could marry anyone. Sneha told me not to worry. She was nice but I didn't know how much I could trust her. What if she went and reported back to her Dad? After all it was his fault too. Mum was discussing a lot of things with Uncle Mahesh. I was a bit scared that she might talk to him about me and Sunny and the baby. I stayed up as long as I could to listen in on their discussions but then I decided to call it a day.

The next day Sneha and I went out shopping to the village shops. The village shops were quite small but they were nice. There were a lot of sari shops and shoe shops. I brought a few new outfits and some sandals to wear. As we shopped Sneha started asking me questions about the night before.

'I heard about you having a boyfriend in the UK.'

I looked at her, how did she find out? I didn't have to guess who had told her, it was obvious that Gran had opened her big mouth again.

'Yes, but who told you that?'

'Well, last night your Gran and Mum were talking to my mum and dad about you'.

I started to get a bit more concerned as to what Mum and Gran had actually told them about me.

'Gran was saying that you needed to get married here quickly because there were rumours going around that you were pregnant. She said you were getting a bit too westernised and forgetting your culture.'

I was shocked; I knew she would stir up trouble.

'So, were you pregnant, Priya?' asked Sneha politely.

I didn't know what to say.

'Yes, I was,' I said quietly.

'Who was the father, if you don't mind me asking?'

I don't really know what made me tell her, but somehow I felt that I could trust her, so I told her.

'His name's Sunny, well Sundip Rai is his real name.'

'Sundip Rai, isn't that a Punjabi name?'

'Yeah, he's Punjabi''

'Is your mum OK about you seeing a Punjabi, because I wouldn't be allowed to see anybody, not of another culture or caste?'

'Well she doesn't know; I hid it from her. If she knew then she wouldn't agree I suppose. I love Sunny a lot. He means the world to me.'

'But it's wrong for a Hindu to marry a Punjabi, because he's not your religion.'

'Look, I was brought up in UK and there we have all different races. I didn't plan to fall in love with a Punjabi, it just happened, you know love.'

'So what's happening with you and Sunny now?'

'I'm still seeing him if that's what you're asking.'

'Your mum mentioned that you just had an abortion before you came here.'

'Oh great, so she's told your family everything about me, how wonderful! How am I suppose to walk around here knowing that everyone knows what's been happening in my life! Maybe I should pack my bags and head back home.'

'Don't be upset.'

'I'm not upset, I just feel like killing the lot of them!'

'It's not your fault,' said Sneha. 'You're not really going, are you?' she said looking worried. I looked up at her and smiled.

'No, of course not, it's not that simple. You know Sneha; you're very different, not like the others.'

She smiled.

'You must be very upset that you had to have an abortion.'

I looked at her, and I paused. '... umm...'

'Come on, let's talk about your wedding; so tell me Sneha, what's his name?'

'Oh, Yash.'

'That's a nice name, isn't it?'

'Yes, he's a nice guy.'

'So how did you and Yash meet?'

'Oh we just met a few weeks ago. He came to see me and he liked me, and I liked him. So we said yes.'

'How do you know what he's really like, I mean have you been out with him and spent some time knowing each other?'

'No, not really, in India it's different, my dad already knows their family. His dad's got a good reputation. Before I even saw him Dad had found out what Yash was doing, what he was like and that.'

'So, are you happy?'

'Of course.'

'You are very lucky Sneha. I just can't understand how you can marry someone without knowing them properly.'

'It's a matter of trust and faith in our parents. I think you should find someone here too, Priya.'

'I can't because I'm... umm.'

'What is it Priya, tell me?'

Then I just said it, 'I'm still pregnant, Sneha.'

Sneha's face changed colour as I told her. She put her hand by her mouth.

'You're pregnant! How? I thought you said...'

'No, I couldn't, that day when I went to see the doctor, I saw this baby in the waiting room. Her mum sat by me, she wasn't that older than me about a year older if anything. She wanted to go to the reception desk to ask the receptionist something; she asked if I could hold her baby for a few seconds as she was all alone. I couldn't say no, so I held her son. When I held him, I couldn't believe it; he was so cute and lovely. It made me think that what I was about to do was totally wrong. I was going to kill an innocent baby that was growing inside me. I just couldn't do it Sneha. When the mother came back we started talking, she told me about her son Liam who she had at 16. I couldn't believe how well she was managing the situation. She said it was a hard decision to make but that it was the best decision she had ever made because she couldn't see life without Liam today. When I went inside to see the doctor I just felt that what I was doing was very wrong. So I didn't terminate the pregnancy.'

'So what are you going to do? They'll soon find out when you start to show,' said Sneha worriedly.

'I know but for the time being I have to keep it quiet and you have to as well. Promise me that you will not say a thing to anyone.'

'I promise,' said Sneha, she hugged me. 'You're so brave you know.'

The day had arrived for Sneha to get married and it was a wedding to remember. Sneha looked so beautiful in her red sari. The cameramen and the photographers had all come and were videoing her. The atmosphere was out of the ordinary. I now understood why they said weddings in India were better than those in the UK by far. It was because the atmosphere said it all. There was a music band, which was fantastic to watch and there were loads of people dancing as they walked towards the wedding hall. When Yash arrived you should have heard the noise as they walked towards the hall. They walked in very slowly. Sneha garlanded Yash to welcome him. They then sat opposite each other as people came to give them presents. The priest conducted the ceremony and Sneha and Yash went around the sacred fire. Yash placed a beautiful mangal sutra around Sneha's neck and put red tilak in her head as a mark that he was her husband.

I really enjoyed the wedding. I wore a beautiful beige and red coloured sari. The lady who did Sneha's makeup did mine too. I also had lots of photos taken with Sneha. A lot of guys who had come were looking at me. I tried hard not to look at them but they just kept staring at me. When the wedding was over and it was time to say farewell to Sneha everyone was crying. I was upset to see Sneha leave too but I knew I would still see her, as Yash didn't live too far from the village.

The next day some of us went to Sneha's in-laws to bring her back home, as it was a wedding tradition. Mum and Sneha's dad had arranged for me to see a few guys and, just to keep everyone happy, I went and met them. There was no one I particularly fancied; I already had Sunny but how could I make them understand that. How could I love another guy? I didn't see any harm in just looking and talking to them; at least Mum wouldn't think I wasn't trying. The guys in India were a different kettle of fish altogether. They spoke very little English and they just didn't meet my standards.

CHAPTER 9

The one thing I liked since I had arrived in India was the feeling that all the stress had gone from my head. I hadn't fallen ill as Mum was very careful about what we ate, she boiled the water on a daily basis and made sure we ate only what was cooked at home. She told me to stay away from junk food and outside food. I wanted to take Sunny a gift as I knew he would be pleased but I wasn't sure what to get him. I asked Sneha what she thought I should buy, Sneha wasn't too sure. She told me she would look around for something I could take back for him. I still had a lot of time to get him something so I wasn't too worried.

Mum was getting a bit annoyed that I kept turning all the guys down. She had only one thing on her mind now and that was to marry me off before we went back to UK. When Mum and I were alone, Mum had the perfect opportunity to speak to me.

'Priya, I need you to get married here before we head back. You know I'm on my own and to marry a daughter off isn't easy. Here I've got Uncle Mahesh and all his family. I am not forcing you to marry just any guy but I want you to choose someone who is going to make you happy. You know it's hard to find a guy in the UK and especially after everything that's happened. Please try and understand what I'm trying to tell you.'

Whilst Mum was talking Sneha arrived with Yash, so we had to end the conversation. It didn't take long for Sneha to get into the kitchen and start helping her mum with the dinner. Yash sat with Uncle in the front room while Sneha and I gossiped in the back. I told Sneha how glad I was to see her and that Mum had been giving me a lecture about marriage just before she had arrived. As we were talking a guy had come to see me. I nudged Sneha to go and persuade her dad that I wasn't interested. Sneha didn't know what to do. She went to find her mum, but came running back.

'Priya, this guy's really good-looking, you're bound to like him.'

'I'm just not interested, Sneha.'

'Just take a look, Priya,' she said excitedly.

She grabbed my arm to show me from the kitchen what he looked like, I took a glance at this guy that she was showing me.

I stopped and went over to the door to have a closer look; he was definitely good looking. Then I sighed, I mean, what was the point, I was pregnant, and I loved Sunny. I didn't know this guy; as far as I was concerned he was a total stranger. Just as I was going into the kitchen, Uncle Mahesh grabbed my arm and took me into the room where he was sitting. The guy was sitting with two other lads. I felt stupid just standing there. I quickly sat down next to Uncle Mahesh who introduced me to him. I was quite embarrassed as I was the centre of attention and all eyes were on me. Sneha's mum brought in some tea. After they had all had some tea Sneha's mum took me into the front to speak to the guy. I hesitated but she wouldn't take no for an answer.

'Just talk to him, you've got nothing to lose,' she said.

I stood outside alone with this guy. I didn't know what to say, I mean what could I say? He spoke gently.

'Hi, my name's Raj, and yours?'

He held his hand out to shake it with mine. Somehow I was quite reluctant. But after a while I shook hands and smiled at him. He spoke good English, which truly amazed me. So far all the guys I had spoken to didn't speak much English at all.

'Hi, my name's Priyanka,' I said. 'But most people call me Priya.'

'That's nice, so what do you do, Priya?'

'I'm at college studying for my A levels.'

'So you aren't working?'

'No, not yet.'

He didn't look very happy when I said I wasn't working. Anyway it didn't matter; it wasn't as if I was going to marry him.

'Don't you want to ask me anything,' he said looking at me?'

I looked at him, what could I ask him?

'Look, I know you're a nice guy and that but I don't want

to get married just yet. I didn't come to India to get married.'

'Why? Don't you like me?'

'It's not that, I'm just not ready OK. I'm only seventeen; I don't plan to marry for at least a good few years yet.'

'Girls here marry at this age. It's a good age to marry and settle down quite early.'

'Well, I don't really agree.'

'When I saw you, I really liked you, and if anything, I want to marry you.'

'You hardly know me, believe me, I'm not the right girl for you; you don't know anything about me. I've got a past, which I don't think you're going to like. You can find someone really nice here. Why bother with someone like me.'

'Because I like you, besides I don't want another girl. I see something in your eyes which makes me feel crazy about you.'

I didn't know what to say. His words were so flattering that I began to feel a spark in my heart for him.

I looked at him. He was just staring at me, so much so that, for the first time, I had time to look at him properly and see what he really looked like. All the other guys that I was told to see, I hadn't really looked at them, not to the extent that I had looked at Raj now. He was quite a handsome chap. His hair was spiked slightly from the top and his eyes shone like the moon. He wasn't clean-shaven; he had a stubbly beard. He was quite fair and I just loved the way he spoke. His voice wasn't deep but had a tone which made you want to talk to him. His body was very toned as though he regularly exercised at the gym. He wore a white short-sleeved shirt with a black design on the back, and tight-fitted jeans. He wore a nice after-shave, which had lingered where I stood, he smelled absolutely gorgeous. For once someone had captured my heart. I don't know how he did it but I was falling for his charismatic looks and his charming words.

'Why are you being so stubborn for, I've already got a boyfriend?' I said bluntly.

I nearly blurted out that I was pregnant too, but I couldn't say that in case he told Uncle.

'Look, so what, after we marry, you'll forget him. A lot of guys here have a girl, but after marriage it's all forgotten. It's youth; of course you're going to have a boyfriend. It's the same here in India too, you know.'

'Why don't you understand? It's not that you've known me for a long time, we've only just met each other; how can you talk about love when you've only just met me?'

'Look, I just admire you and I think you're very beautiful. I don't know how but you've captured my heart. I've already fallen in love with you. What is it that you say in London?'

'Love at first sight,' I said smiling at him.

'That's it, love at first sight.'

I couldn't help smiling at what he was saying, he was a real charmer. There was something about him which made me forget Sunny for a minute or two. I felt I was holding onto his conversation because I wanted too. I could have said no and walked off, but I didn't.

Then the most embarrassing thing happened, as I

started to walk off the heel of my sandal got stuck in the tiled floor. It was stuck fast and my whole shoe came off. I felt so uncomfortable. I could feel my skin turning red with embarrassment. Raj smiled and came over. He freed my sandal effortlessly.

'Here,' he said as he passed it to me, and, as he did so, he touched my hand. My heart started to race, it was uncontrollable. I just couldn't put a leash on it. I took a deep breath and took my sandal and put it on.

I didn't know what to say, I smiled and we both started to laugh.

'I tell you what Priya, how would you like to go on a tour tomorrow in Dandi. I'll show you all the sights from my bike you'll love it. Then you can decide for yourself whether you like me or not, no pressure, I promise.'

'I won't change my mind; you know that,' I said smiling. I agreed to meet him the next day for a tour.

When he had left, Sneha who was still there wanted to know what had happened. I filled her in and she was very excited for me.

'Priya, I think he's the one for you.' She said laughing aloud.

I looked at her, 'I don't think so.' Then we both started laughing.

The next day, I woke up quite early; I bathed and put on a nice Asian top with my jeans. I can't say I didn't make any effort, in fact I had. I tied my hair up and applied loads of foundation and make-up to make my skin look spotless and clean.

At 9.00 am sharp Raj pulled up on his bike. He had a beautiful red and black Honda bike. I was a bit anxious about how I would sit on it; I hadn't sat on a bike before. He came in and spoke to Uncle briefly. He then came up to me, and remarked how beautiful I looked. I could feel myself going bright red.

'Shall we leave then?' he asked.

'Alright,' I said eagerly.

I saw Mum smiling from the doorway. Everyone laughed as we both left on the bike. Raj helped me onto the bike. I was quite nervous and as he drove off I automatically grabbed his waist with both hands. I was terrified! I sat behind silently as he drove. He was laughing as he looked through his side mirror and saw my face; I must have looked like I had seen a ghost.

'Are you scared, Priya?' he asked.

'Yes, what do you think?' I said aloud.

'Just hold on tight and you'll be fine.'

'Don't worry I have no intention in letting go right now.' He laughed.

At first I closed my eyes and then I slowly opened them. After a while I started enjoying the ride. I looked up and I could feel the wind, it felt good. That day, Raj took me around showing me all the sights. At lunchtime, he took me to a nice restaurant to eat which was really nice. I was a bit cautious about eating out but Raj said it was a very clean restaurant. The restaurant was small, and Raj cleverly picked a table right in the corner, which was cut off from all the other tables. He sat opposite me looking directly into my eyes. I was feeling quite uneasy as he just stared at me. Luckily the drinks arrived which helped break the silence between us. I held onto the glass and as we talked he kept touching my hand, which made me really nervous and on edge. Raj had ordered Masala Dosa an Indian dish made of a pancake with a vegetarian filling inside, when the food arrived I quickly tucked into it. It was very nice and he also ordered Almond Ice-cream for desert which was also very tasty. Soon I had forgotten everything and was enjoying his company. I hadn't felt this good in ages. We laughed and joked, he was telling me a load of stories about things that had happened to him.

The day went so quickly that before I knew it was 7.00pm. I had a massive smile on my face as I walked into the house that evening. I had really enjoyed my day. Raj was real good company. His conversations weren't boring but out of this world. He was such an interesting character, that being with him made me feel really good inside, something which I had never felt with Sunny. He made me feel really special. He took great care of me all day long and if we walked anywhere, where it was rocky or steep he would hold my hand just so that I didn't fall.

That week Raj kept coming over to take me out. He seemed to get around Uncle Mahesh to let me go out with him. Soon I was waiting for him to arrive. Everyday I made an immense effort to look attractive and each day he commented how beautiful I looked. I was enjoying myself so much that I had forgotten about Sunny and the baby I was carrying. It was only when Sneha mentioned it when she came over that I was brought back to reality. Then I realised that I shouldn't be doing this to Raj but I had started to like Raj more than I could imagine. I never felt so good within myself. I didn't really know what to do.

That night Mum asked me what I thought about marrying Raj. She said that his parents had asked about me. I didn't know what to say. Sneha kept nudging me to say yes. I was in a big dilemma because Raj didn't know anything about the baby. I knew there was no way Mum was going to get me married to Sunny. If anything I could marry Raj and keep everybody happy, so after a lot of thought I agreed. Mum and Gran were over the moon as was Uncle Mahesh; she hugged me and went to tell Gran and everyone else.

The preparations for the wedding were all underway as we were heading home at the end of the week. Sneha had come over to stay for a few days as her dad asked her to help with the wedding preparations. Uncle Mahesh suggested that we should all go to Mumbai to buy saris for the wedding. There was no waiting around. I was off to Mumbai with Sneha and Yash, and Mum and Uncle Mahesh to do some serious shopping for my wedding. Sneha took me to all the good sari shops. We saw so many beautiful outfits. Then I came across this one that really stood out from the rest. I had to buy it. The next few days were very busy. We had loads of people coming over and singing songs about Raj and me. It was kind of funny; all the preparations were underway for the wedding. I had three days of pithi, where I was covered with this yellow paste. A girl from the village came to put mehndi on my hands and feet. Before I knew it, I was getting married!

I was very nervous. A lady came from the beauty parlour to do my makeup. When I was all dressed up, Sneha took me to the room where everyone was gathered. Mum got all emotional as soon as she saw me all dressed up in my wedding outfit. The morning was quite hectic; once the pre-wedding ceremony was performed, we had lunch and a photographer took photos of me. I felt a bit stupid doing all these different poses. The time came for the groom to arrive; we could hear loud music and loads of bangers going off as they approached the wedding hall. I was quite excited. Sneha was with me throughout which helped me feel more relaxed.

Soon Raj had arrived into the hall. I was excited and my heart was racing. I was anxious to see what he looked like in his wedding clothes. I could hear some girls screaming nearby saying the groom looked hot. Then I was asked to go outside to greet him. They gave me a garland that I was supposed to go and place around Raj. Sneha came with me. It was really scary but exciting at the same time. Loads of people had gathered and there were so many people who had come with Raj. I only knew what I had to do because I had just seen Sneha get married. I walked slowly towards Raj who stood a distance away from me. I walked with my head down, my hands were trembling. When I reached him I put the garland carefully around his neck. He quietly whispered,

'Hi sundari, you look very beautiful.'

I smiled and felt deeply embarrassed, I then walked back inside. I could feel my hands turn wet with perspiration.

'What did he say, what did he say?' Asked Sneha excitedly.

'He said I was looking hot,' I said smiling at her.

The wedding went as planned and that night I went back to Raj's house. The wedding didn't really scare me but the fact I was now married and was going to spend my first night with Raj did! Somehow Sunny kept coming into my head. Up to now the thought of being with Sunny was hardly in my mind but the three weeks were nearly up and I knew when I went back home I would have to face the music. I spent a few days with Raj before I returned home with Mum and Gran.

Raj came to drop me off at the airport. He was quite tearful all the way and, he held onto my hand tightly. I was quite tearful as I had to leave. I noticed a tear in his eye too. He handed me a small gift box and an envelope which he told me not to open until I got home. I hugged him tightly and then left him standing with a few of his mates who had come along. I was really upset as I said my farewells to Raj. The last three weeks had been so wonderful that I was really sad to leave. I never thought that I would feel like this. I never imagined that in three weeks I would be so attached to anyone as I was to Raj.

I slept the whole way on the flight back to the UK, maybe because it was night time when we left India. I was thinking a lot about my health too, which I hadn't really paid a lot of attention to while I was in India. I never asked the doctor if I could travel but I presumed that it was safe to do so anyway. It wasn't as if I was really that big and heavily pregnant. The weather had been so warm in India that as we were approaching England I felt really cold? Somehow I wasn't looking forward to coming back home, for many reasons but I knew that I didn't have much choice.

CHAPTER 10

Priya's pregnant (12-16 weeks)

We arrived back in the UK on Sunday. The last three weeks seemed to be like a dream. I had only gone to India to attend a wedding not come back as a bride myself. I felt my brain had been brainwashed for the last few weeks, but was now functioning properly again. I was really scared as to what I was going to tell Sunny. I knew that he would ring me sometime today. I turned my phone off so that I wouldn't have to answer his calls.

Aunt Neelam and her family were all waiting at the house congratulating me on my marriage. It felt really strange. I had tied the knot and that was it. As soon as I landed in the UK I felt my stress levels start to rise again. Mum had already given her the good news while we were India. She gave me a big hug and congratulated me on tying the knot with Raj. Whilst Aunt Neelam talked with Mum I sneaked upstairs to open my post that had piled up over the last three weeks. There was a letter for me to see the midwife and an appointment for me to have a scan too. I had also received my free maternity exemption card which enabled me to get free prescriptions and dental check-ups. I was now 13 weeks pregnant. I have to say I wasn't feeling ill or anything, in fact I could hardly tell that I was pregnant, but lately I noticed that I had a lot of energy within me.

Everyone sat and chatted about the wedding. Aunt Neelam sat holding the wedding album. Karim and Sahil kept on teasing me about being married. I still had mehndi on my hands and feet. It was starting to fade away but very slowly. My colour had changed to a really dark brownie colour. I noticed the ring on my finger and I began to feel on edge, so after Aunty left I went upstairs to unpack my bags and think about what to do. The first thing I took out of my suitcase was the small gift box and envelope that Raj had given me. I opened the envelope which contained a lovely photo of us that we had taken at a studio and a letter, which read:

My darling wife Priya,

You just don't know how much I am already missing you. Without you here, life seems to be dull. I love you so much and cannot wait to join you in the UK. You're my princess who I always dreamt off. I hope you like the small gift that I have given you; it will remind you of me wherever you go. Please wear it and accept it as a token of my love. I miss you so much meri jaan. I don't know how I'm going to spend the coming days without you. Say hello to everyone for me. I love you.
Raj

I opened the gift box; it was a beautiful heart-shaped locket. I opened the locket which had a small picture of us inside. It was beautiful. I put it around my neck straight away. I looked at our photo and kissed Raj on the lips. I really did love him. My love for him wasn't fake but true. If anything my feelings for Sunny seemed to have faded away. I stood by the mirror admiring the locket. I took out all the new outfits I had brought with Sneha. I was glad that I had married him, my feelings for Raj were getting stronger and stronger, and as I started to unpack I decided to call Rina. I switched my mobile back on. There was a text message from Sunny. I opened it to see what he had written,

Hi Priya,
*   Where R U, give me a call baby. I've really missed u.*
Love U Sunny.

I felt I was digging a bigger and bigger hole, first the baby, then the wedding and now Sunny. This was becoming a right nightmare. The phone started to ring; Mum answered it from downstairs.

'Priya, it's for you, it's Raj!' She shouted.

'I'll take it from here, Mum.' I picked up the cordless.

'Hello.'

'Hi Priya, it's me, Raj, how are you?'

'I'm fine.'

'When did you arrive home?'

'A few hours ago.'

'I thought you might ring me?'

'Well I was going to but we've had so many visitors, that I couldn't ring straight away. I'm really sorry.'

'It's OK, so, how are you?'

'Umm good, just unpacking my suitcase and that. I really loved the locket you gave me, thank you so much. I've already put it on, thanks Raj for such a wonderful gift.'

'I'm glad you like it, so do you miss me?'

'Of course I do, and do you miss me?'

'I miss you so much, meri jaan that being without you seems like there's nothing else for me to live for. I didn't think it was going to be this difficult to live without you. You know I picked up the application form from Bombay for me to come over, I will fill it in but I need you to send me some documents. I'll phone and let you know what they are, OK.'

'I forgot about that, well just tell me what documents you need and I'll send them over.'

'So how's my beautiful wife? You sound a bit quiet on the phone.'

'No, it's just that it's been a long flight and I'm a bit tired and that.'

'Well I'd better let you go then, I'll phone you again tomorrow, OK sweetheart? Look after yourself, I love you.'

'I love you too, bye.'

I had to think real. I was now married and soon everyone was going to know. Maybe I should show everyone that I was married. I mean I couldn't really hide that could I. The big secret I had hidden was scaring me to bits inside. The mangal sutra which Raj had placed around my neck said it all. The ring and mangal sutra kept on reminding me that I was now married. Tomorrow I had to go to college and there was no way I could go wearing the mangal sutra and wedding ring. Everyone would notice that I got married, and what would Sunny say? I had to tell Sunny but I couldn't just shock him on the first day of me arriving back at college. I had to do it gradually.

I called Rina on the mobile.

'Hi Rina, it's me, Priya.'

'Oh hi Priya, when did you get back?'

'A few hours ago.'

'So, how was it, your trip to India?'

'Oh really good.'

'And the wedding?'

'Oh great.'

'So would you go again then?'

'Sure why not, I really enjoyed myself.'

'There's something else I need to tell you,' I said quietly. 'I got married while I was there.'

'Did you say you got married?'

'Yes, I got married.'

'That's great Priya, but don't you think you're a bit young to get tied down? Were you forced and that because of … you know?'

'No! I don't know. Well Uncle Mahesh and Mum

insisted that I see some guys. I didn't intend to get married but then I saw this guy called Raj who wouldn't take no for an answer. Mind you he's really something you know.'

'Seems like you like this guy.'

'He's very nice you know, not like Sunny – immature, Raj's quite mature and he seems to make all the moves which I like in a man. I don't know but with Sunny I'm always running after him, he's not what you call responsible, just I suppose good looking and that.'

'That's a bit of a change of tune isn't it Priya? One minute it was all Sunny this and Sunny that and now there's no one like Raj. Does Sunny know?'

'I haven't spoken to Sunny yet, please don't say anything to him, I'll tell him in my own good time.'

'After all you have been with him for a long while.'

'Maybe I thought I was in love with him but I think it can't have been love, just a crush. Raj is so different, he's a real man.'

'I thought you loved Sunny?'

'I do, but... Forget it, look, I'm married and that's that. I've got to go; I'll see you tomorrow at college.'

'You've done the right thing Priya, take care, bye.'

That evening we all sat in the living room watching the wedding cassette. It was fun, sitting and watching my wedding. It was nice to see Raj. If anything Mum was now happy to know that I was married. Sahil and Karim had come too. They were making all these weird noises as Raj came on screen.

'It's the Bollywood couple!' shouted Karim. 'I never thought you had a taste for men from India.'

'Neither did I until I went over.'

'Must be something in the water; maybe someone did a bit of magic on you and you fell in love.'

'Come on guys, this isn't a joke you know.'

'We've got to go now; Mum must be waiting for us,' said Sahil. Say hello to Raja Hindustani from us.'

I smiled.

'Of course I will.'

'See you later sis.'

Mum knew that I couldn't really mess around now that I was married. I didn't know how I was feeling inside, I felt mixed up. I *was* happy; I definitely loved Raj more than I did Sunny. I still loved Sunny but not like I used too, maybe even if I tried to ignore the fact that Sunny didn't mean a thing to me now, it wasn't going to go away that easily. I wasn't sure how I felt about Sunny now. I still felt something for him, but I was now someone else's. Sunny didn't have a right to me anymore. I knew I would have to stop messing around with him.

For some reason I was feeling really scared and worried inside about the baby and it was causing me to have a lot of sleepless nights thinking that the baby might be abnormal. It was a worry, which was constantly in the back of my mind, and I think it was because I saw a Down Syndrome baby at the doctor's surgery and it scared me into wondering what if my baby was like that too. I couldn't really cope with something like that. That night I logged onto my computer; I hadn't checked my email for three weeks. Anita had sent me a message.

Hi Priya

I'm really worried about you. One minute you're pregnant, the next you're flying to India. What's going on, what are you up to? What happened with the pregnancy, why didn't you mention anything in your last email? Write soon. I'm really worried.
Yrs Anita

I had a lot of explaining to do to Anita. I thought for a while what I was going to write to her. I never lied to Anita that was why I didn't mention the pregnancy in my last email to her. I began typing,

Hi Anita

I'm back from India now. Had a wonderful time and enjoyed Sneha's wedding.

I know I left without saying much because I couldn't lie to you. I'm still pregnant, but everyone thinks that I've had an abortion. I know you're going to go mad but I couldn't do it Anita.

Do you want to hear more? I've got married to a man called Raj from India? Tell me I'm losing it! I know everything's really messed up. I lied in the beginning but now I feel the whole things just gone out of hand and I can't stop it.

I didn't go to India to marry but Mum wanted me

to marry someone, but I sort of fell in love with Raj and although I tried to tell him that I was already involved with someone else he didn't really want to know. I don't know what's going to happen now, but that's the picture so far about me. Sorry Anita, I know I've messed up.
Priya

The next day at college I caught up with Sunny, first thing in the morning. He hugged me and kissed my cheek. I felt very uncomfortable. I tried to push him away gently.

'Hey babes, what's up? Have I done something?'

'No, I'm fine, just you know.'

'So did you have a good time and that in India?'

'Yeah, it was great.'

'So where's my kiss, I haven't had one for weeks.'

'Not now Sunny, everyone's watching.'

'You're looking very hot, Priya since you came back.'

'Oh, here comes Rina. I'll catch up with you later Sunny, I have to go, I've got Maths.'

'Hey Priya, what's up? You're acting all weird and that.'

'It's not me; it's you who's acting all weird. I'll talk to you later, bye.'

This was going to be harder than I thought. I mean, how was I going to stop Sunny from getting close to me? He always grabbed me and cuddled me and all that stuff and of course, I couldn't do that with him anymore. As I walked with Rina to my lesson, she questioned me about why I had really gone and got married. I didn't have an answer to her question. I don't even know myself why I had got married. The only thing that came to my mind was that I wanted to see Mum happy. I knew that she would now be happy knowing that I was safely married. It was a responsibility off her shoulders. Maybe I owed her that much at least. The big question that kept on going round and round in my head was the baby. It wasn't how I had planned my life. But then I never planned to getting married either did I? Maybe life never ever did go as planned. I just had to go with the flow. It wasn't as if I hated Raj, if anything I really loved him. Rina was very angry with me when I told her that I was still pregnant. She'd thought I had terminated the pregnancy too.

I now had to see the midwife every four weeks to make sure the pregnancy was going OK. Each time I went the midwife would carry out various tests. She would start by measuring my blood pressure and then dip a stick into my urine sample to make sure I didn't have any sugar or protein in it. She would then check what my weight was. Last of all I had to lie on the bed and put my t-shirt up while she checked my abdomen. I was also sent to have some blood tests done to check that there weren't any abnormalities in the baby. I didn't realise there were so many things to look out for when you were pregnant.

CHAPTER 11

I had an appointment at the hospital for my first ultrasound scan; however, I really didn't know how long it was going to take. The hospital was a bit of a journey from my house. I really didn't want to go alone so I asked Rina if she would come with me to the hospital but she couldn't come. I didn't quite believe her as ever since I told her about my pregnancy I noticed she was acting differently towards me as if she didn't really want anything to do with me anymore. I couldn't really blame her.

I told Mum that I was attending a conference at a university as part of my course. I had to catch two buses to get me to the hospital. I hated buses, if anything it made me feel sicker. When I got to the hospital I wasn't very sure where to go. It was a massive hospital that had several different parts to it. I eventually asked someone who told me where to go. When I went inside I saw the reception desk so I waited in the queue and then showed her the scan letter. She gave me some directions which I thought I understood but when I got to where she had told me I found out that I had somehow ended up in Imaging A which was x-rays, I began to feel anxious, I looked at the time and could see my appointment time had passed by. I started panicking and started to ask for help. Luckily I met a nice man who showed me where to go. I don't really know how I ended up where I did.

When I got there I handed my letter to a nurse. She looked at it and picked up that I was late. I explained to her that I had got lost and that but she didn't seem too happy about that. She told me to take a seat and said I would have to wait a bit longer as I was late. The letter stated clearly that I should go with a full bladder but I wasn't someone who could walk around with a full bladder. After coming back from the loo I started sipping on the mineral water I had brought along with me. As I waited I could see all eyes were on me. I felt a bit intimidated by this. Everyone in the waiting room was much older than me and they all had their partners with them. Here I was all alone and without anyone. I felt kind of stupid and just didn't feel like I belonged here. I could hear this woman whispering to her boyfriend saying,

'She's a bit young to have a baby isn't she?'

Her boyfriend told her to be quiet.

I went and sat in another seating area where there were less people. I felt like a school kid. It was true because everyone at college said I didn't look my age. I looked about sixteen because of my height and frame. I bet everyone was wondering what I was doing here. Just then a nurse called my name out. I quickly got up and walked over to her. She directed me to the scan room. I went inside excitedly; I mean today I was going to see the baby that was growing inside of me for the first time. The sonographer told me to take my shoes off and to lie on the bed. I lay down and rolled up my t-shirt. She then put some gel onto my tummy which was very cold. She moved a transducer, as she called it, over my tummy to view the baby. Then she said,

'You don't seem to have drunk enough water. You need to have a full bladder for this otherwise we can't see the baby properly.'

I felt quite stupid, I mean how could I tell her that I did come to the hospital with a full bladder but was unable to keep it in? I quickly sat up and galloped a whole bottle of water until I felt like I was bursting again for the loo. I lay down again and the sonographer applied more gel onto my stomach. I turned my head on the side to see the screen.

'That's better; I can now see the baby.'

Seeing the baby on the screen was really amazing, something which I had never seen before or could have imagined. It wasn't that clear but you could make out that it was what looked like a baby. It was all curled up. After the sonographer had finished doing the scan she gave me some tissues to wipe the gel off with. I got up and put my shoes on. She asked if I would like to buy a copy of the scan photo. I was dead excited and said yes. As I walked out of the hospital I had a big smile on my face as I held the scan photo in my hand. Although I was so excited about it I didn't really have anyone to enjoy this moment of joy with which made me feel really down again.

What was the point when there was no one to enjoy your joy and happiness? If Mum knew she would be so happy but how could I tell her so soon.

As I headed home I phoned the doctors to see if my blood test results had come through. This was something I was really worried about. It was the tests to check for abnormalities in the baby. I kept ringing but couldn't get through. I eventually decided to go down to the doctors as I had plenty of time on my hands and Mum wasn't expecting me to be back until late. When I got there the receptionist was a bit rude because I hadn't made an appointment to see the midwife. I tried explaining to her that I didn't really need to see the midwife, that all I had come for was my blood test results. She had this face on her but anyway she managed to dig through my file to see if the results had come.

'Oh yes, they've come.'

'And?'

'Well it doesn't say anything, oh sorry it does. They're fine, nothing abnormal.

'What does that mean?'

'That you've got nothing to worry about, any more questions?' she said looking angrily at me.

'No, there's no need for you to shout, I was only asking.'

Despite her rudeness, I was so relieved to hear her say that.

'I'll get some sleep tonight after all the worry,' I thought.

CHAPTER 12

Priya's pregnant
(16-20 weeks)

I decided to tell Sunny the truth about Raj. I didn't know how he would react but I had to tell him. I phoned and asked him to meet me at the park after college finished. I walked by myself to the park to meet him.

I sat on the bench waiting for him to arrive. Soon I saw him come running up. He didn't say much, he just sat down. I could tell he knew that something was up.

'I've got to tell you something Sunny,' I said.

'I gathered that, because you've been acting really weird since you've been back. I don't know whether I've done something to you or what? Maybe you can shed some light.'

'I don't really know how to tell you this but I can't see you anymore.'

'Oh, I see, so you've found someone else have you?'

'Well yes, but it's not like that.'

'So how is it, you tell me Priya! So the two years we've been together hasn't meant a damn thing to you. Oh, I forgot you only used me to have someone to hang around with and to tell all your soppy stories to about your dad.'

'Stop it Sunny! Try and understand will you!'

I started to cry as I just couldn't get it out of me that I was married. Then I showed him my hand. Sunny just stood looking straight down at my hand.

'You're married!'

I nodded.

He started shaking me vigorously.

'To who Priya and when? Damn it, answer me! To who?'

I started to cry again,

'I got married in India, Sunny.'

I could see the anger and hurt in Sunny's eyes.

'So that's it. We're finished, that's what you came to tell me?'

'I didn't want to Sunny, but I didn't have any choice.'

'I don't want to know Priya, I couldn't care less! You hear me, I don't care!'

He ran off leaving me in the park all by myself.

All the way home I cried. I couldn't believe I had just ended whatever we had. As soon as I walked back in the house I started crying on Mum's shoulder. She asked me what was wrong, but I couldn't tell her. Right now all I needed was comfort, my mother's love. As I cried and cried I started to feel light-headed. Before I knew it I had collapsed. I didn't get up straight away; in fact when I got up I could see that I was in an ambulance going to hospital. I still didn't feel OK. When I woke up later I was taken into casualty. I was soon given a bed while I waited for a doctor to come and examine me. After a while a team of doctors had come. They asked Mum and Gran to wait in the waiting room while they examined me. The doctors shut the curtains around my bed. I was feeling scared seeing so many young doctors around me.

'Hi Priya, my name's Doctor Caroline. How are you feeling?'

'OK, thank you.'

'So, can you tell me what happened?'

I explained how I suddenly felt light-headed and must have passed out. The doctor felt my pulse and checked my blood pressure, which was low. She then asked,

'Are you pregnant?'

I nodded, 'yes, I am.'

'Well, that explains everything.'

Then she examined my stomach and felt the baby. She checked the baby's heartbeat. She then told me that she was going to send me for a scan to see if the baby was OK.

After a short while I was taken to a different part of the hospital for a scan. Thankfully everything was OK. The doctor said that I was a bit dehydrated too and needed to drink plenty of fluids. She started opening the curtains. Mum quickly appeared out of nowhere.

'Is everything OK, doctor?' she asked.

'Yes, don't worry, your daughter's fine and so is the baby. We'll discharge you sometime this evening. Have you any questions?'

'Umm no,' I replied quietly, waiting for Mum to react.

From the corner of my eye I could see Mum and Gran listening to what the doctor had just said, they both looked at each other. I didn't know what they were thinking. There was no smile on either of their faces but a puzzled look, like things didn't add up.

'Pregnant?' said Mum, confused. 'You and Raj?' she said looking straight at me.

I had to lie; I couldn't say it was Sunny's baby. I nodded.

'Yes, Mum.'

She seemed relieved when I said it was Raj's. Then they both smiled. Mum came over and held my hand. 'You get some rest.'

I closed my eyes and fell asleep for a while.

When I woke up I could hear Mum and Gran talking about me. I kept my eyes closed to hear what they were saying. They were talking about my pregnancy. Gran was questioning how I could possibly get pregnant so soon after my marriage. I felt really worried hearing them talking. Mum didn't really listen to her, she told her that I had already had the abortion and that this was Raj's baby. She told Gran not to make matters worse by spreading rumours which could cause problems in the house. I was relieved when I heard Mum say that. I quickly opened my eyes, as I knew they would stop talking once I got up.

That evening I was discharged from hospital. The doctor told me to see a midwife. I was glad she didn't mention anything about how many weeks pregnant I was. When we got home, Mum told me to put my feet up. I sat in the lounge while Mum brought me a hot cup of tea and some biscuits. While I was having my tea and biscuits I heard Mum talking on the phone. It was my mother-in-law. Mum had already given her the good news. I was astonished. She could have waited a few days before saying anything. I was more worried about how Raj would now react after knowing the truth. Raj apparently wasn't at home so luckily I didn't have to speak to him. I felt really bad inside. I was worried about how he would take the news; he wasn't stupid. I'm sure that he would work out that I had lied.

Mum drove me to the Health Care Centre as I had an appointment to see the midwife. She sat in the waiting room while I went inside to see the midwife. She checked my blood pressure and urine, which were normal. I was now seventeen weeks pregnant. The midwife told me that any week now I should feel the baby move. I was feeling quite worried about this. I couldn't let anyone at home know that I was so many weeks pregnant. I asked the midwife how much the baby had developed, as I was a bit curious. The midwife was quite nice and explained the growth of the baby. She said that the face was now shaping more to look more human and the fingers and toenails were growing and the baby had now got its own fingerprints.

Although I was happy I was feeling a bit negative about this baby which I hadn't felt up to now. After going to India and marrying Raj my views had somehow changed to what I now felt. My clothes had started to become tight and I had to go and buy looser clothing. You still couldn't tell that I was pregnant as the baggy clothes covered my stomach. I looked at maternity clothes but they weren't very appealing or fashionable. I just brought a few bigger size t-shirts and trousers. My bra size had also gone up and I needed to get some bigger bras. I went to Marks and Spencer to get someone to measure my breasts to see what size I would need. But, for the first time, I started to feel that perhaps I didn't want this baby as much as I thought. My ties with Sunny were now broken and my love for him had all but vanished into thin air. I questioned myself as to whether I had ever really loved him. It felt as if it was just a stupid crush or maybe I did really love him, but not to the point where he meant the world to me.

For the next few days I stayed at home. Mum was pampering me a lot and Gran was making a lot of effort with me which was kind of strange. I felt things were beginning to fall into place. I didn't have to hide in my room all the time now. Mum had already asked me what I intended to do about college now that I was expecting. I really wanted to finish the year off. I knew that uni was out of the question but I knew that I could still finish college and get my grades. I wasn't really looking forward to going back to college though, especially now that Sunny and I had broken up. I just couldn't face him and his mates. I still sort of loved him even though I had married Raj. My main worry right now was what was going through Raj's mind. Since Mum had rang him he hadn't spoken to me. I thought I give him a few days before I rang him.

Priya's pregnant
(20-24 weeks)

I decided to go in on Friday to college. I couldn't afford to miss out on any more lessons. It was really awful seeing Sunny now and then. Each time I passed him he would give me a dirty look. Two of his mates came to ask me why I wasn't speaking to Sunny but I told them to mind their own business. I knew deep down that it was only Sunny that could have sent them; it wasn't as if they didn't know. I guessed that sooner or later he would come around, but things didn't seem to improve over the coming weeks, instead Sunny started hanging around Naila. I think he was showing me that he had forgotten me and moved on but I didn't really believe that, because he was also keeping track of where I was going during the day.

I started going to the library to catch up on my studies. With so much happening in my life I had a lot of work to catch up on. If I weren't careful my grades would definitely suffer. But I noticed that Sunny had also started to hang around the library too. I think he was keeping a tab on what I was up to as well as showing off his new girlfriend, who I thought was much less attractive than me. Each time Sunny came to the library I couldn't help looking at him as he was always with that Naila girl. I don't really know what he saw in her, but I knew she was a right flirt. You should have seen the way she dressed; her skirt was so short that it didn't make much difference whether she wore one or not.

I went to hospital for my twenty-week scan to see if the baby was developing OK. The sonographer said that everything was looking well. I brought the scan photo. This time I had arrived at the right time and had come with a full bladder. I didn't want to make a fool out of myself a second time. Mum waited in the waiting room as I had no choice but to take her as she wouldn't take no for an answer. Having Mum with me gave me that extra bit of confidence and support that I needed. After I had been for my scan I went over to where Mum was sitting and I switched the scan photo with my earlier scan photo so Mum didn't get suspicious about the pregnancy. I knew she wouldn't be able to read the date as she wore glasses and she hadn't brought them with her.

I soon sprang back after the baby started to kick inside me. It was the most exciting and wonderful thing to experience. At first I got scared but then I got really excited. I think if I told my mates at college they would think it was totally gross but when it happens to yourself you can't really explain how wonderful it is. Even if someone else had told me about this I'm sure I would have thought of it being totally disgusting but it was just so nice to know that the baby was so real and kicking.

Mum was quite good when I got home after college. She made me put my feet up and didn't let me do anything in case I hurt myself. I think she was overdoing it a bit, but that's mothers for you. Gran was getting on my nerves a bit, she kept telling Mum that I shouldn't be allowed to go to college in my condition and she was moaning that I should concentrate on other stuff now, like household chores and cooking. I didn't know what had eaten her up but she was being a typical nuisance.

I had another appointment to see the midwife, who told me to book in for antenatal classes at the hospital. I really didn't want to go. I wasn't quite sure what antenatal classes were. I asked the midwife what it was; she laughed at me and explained to me what they were for.

'Priya, these classes are for pregnant women to go and learn how to prepare for the birth, it teaches you breathing exercises and relaxation exercises when you are in labour. It's not just about that, in fact you meet other expectant parents, you also have a chance to talk to a midwife about any worries you may have about the pregnancy, and they will tell you about the different types of pain relief that's available and ways of coping in labour. So you can't afford to miss out on this Priya because it's vital that all pregnant women attend.'

I could see her point of view about going to antenatal classes. I really needed to go; I mean I didn't have a clue about anything. I needed to find out but my main worry was would Raj come with me to the sessions and if he wouldn't who could I take. I know Mum would jump at the chance of coming with me but I didn't want to take my Mum because I would look like an idiot.

I was twenty-three weeks pregnant now. The baby seemed to be growing fine but I had developed something called gestational diabetes which was sugar in my urine. The first few months of my pregnancy was quite normal, however, as the months passed by I was finding I was developing all sorts of problems. I was feeling a bit scared each time I had to pay a visit to the midwife. Since I had sugar in my urine, I was asked to go to the hospital to have a Glucose Tolerance test done and to make matters worse the midwife told me that my blood pressure was quite high, which wasn't good as I could suffer from a condition called pre-eclampsia. The midwife explained that a lot of women got this, as there was a rapid weight gain in the second trimester. She told me not to worry too much as it was quite mild. Mum had stopped me doing literally everything now. I could see from her face that she was really worried about me.

Rumours had gone around college that I was pregnant, I tried acting as though I wasn't but it was becoming harder and harder to hide as my belly seemed to be getting bigger by the day. I had also noticed a big change in Rina too; she had started to avoid me. I think her parents must have told her to keep away from me. I was feeling a bit of a loner. Kez and Lucy had started to act all snobbish with me too. The only one who I found I could talk to was Becky. At first Becky was just one of the girls in my lessons but after she found out that I was pregnant she started to take good care of me. I don't really know how we suddenly got close but as I visited the library more frequently I found that she too spent a great deal of her time revising there.

One day, after Maths ended, Miss Stanley asked me why I hadn't been coming on a regular basis. I didn't know what to say. I decided to tell her the truth; after all she was going to find out sooner or later. Miss Stanley was shocked when I told her. She was really supportive and caring, which was a relief. Later that day I headed off to the library with Becky. We hadn't been there long when Sunny barged up and started screaming at the top of his voice,

'How could you lie to me, Priya!' he shouted.

The librarian was furious and told us to go outside.

I followed him outside to find out what he was shouting about.

'Why are you causing such a big commotion for?'

'So, are you still pregnant?' he screamed.

I was gob-smacked, what could I say?

'Well umm.'

'You don't have to deny it because Smaila and Lucy heard you telling Miss Stanley about it!'

I didn't know what to say. I couldn't lie to him. He started shouting more loudly.

'Tell me, did you or didn't you have the abortion!'

I was going bright red as a group of students had gathered around.

'I didn't have the abortion, alright! '

'I just knew it! I knew rumours were going around but I didn't think that it was true. Well just remember Priya, I'm not going to support you or the child, get that into your thick head, you're all alone in this. By the way I bet you told your so-called husband that it's his baby, haven't you?'

I started walking off, I couldn't hear anymore of this.

'That's it, walk off, I hate you Priya! I hate you! Go to that freshi who you married, that's all you're worth!'

By the time Sunny had finished shouting at me there was a big crowd standing around us. Becky came up to me.

'Is he the father Priya?' she asked.

I nodded, 'yeah he is.'

I started crying as I walked back into the library. I just got my stuff and walked out.

'I'm not coming back, Becky, I quit.'

Becky came up running after me.

'You can't quit now, we haven't got much longer to go!'

'I can't take this anymore. Anyway, what use it, it's not as though I'm going to uni.'

'Think about it tonight Priya, don't make such a hasty decision just because of Sunny.'

'I'm not; I was thinking of quitting anyway, I can't cope with this kind of stress right now.'

I walked off leaving Becky standing by the college gates. That was it, my last day at college.

CHAPTER 14

Priya's pregnant
(24-28 weeks)

When I arrived home, Mum was on the phone to my mother-in-law. I went into the lounge and sat down, my feet and back was aching. Mum came into the lounge, holding the phone.

'Here I'll pass you over to Priya.'

I spoke to my mother-in-law before she passed the phone to Raj. I was feeling really edgy about what to say to him. I hadn't spoken to him since Mum had told them about me being pregnant.

'Hi jaan,' he said.

The line wasn't too clear there was a lot of crackling and echoing.

'Hi love, how are you? Can you hear me, the line isn't very good,' I said.

'Yes, I can hear you, I'm well, but tell me how you are? I hear we have some good news to share.'

I didn't know what to say.

'So is it true that you're expecting?'

'Yes, are you happy?' I asked.

'Well of course I am, I mean I didn't really think we'd scored a goal ... but I presume you'd know if you have or haven't.'

I changed the conversation because I just couldn't lie to him anymore.

'So did you receive all the documents that I sent to you?'

'Oh yes, got them yesterday. I'll start the procedures. Hopefully things should become easier now that we're going to have a baby.'

'I guess so.'

'So, what have you been up to, jaan?'

'Oh nothing much, I've left college.'

'I think that's a good idea, you need to rest and concentrate on the baby now.'

'How many weeks pregnant are you, Priya?'

I was astonished; I didn't expect him to ask me that, I didn't know what to say.

'Umm, I'm not quite sure,' I replied in fright. 'I've got to go; I'll talk to you later.'

I quickly put the phone down. I felt all hot and sweaty. I wondered whether he knew that I was lying to him. He did act as though he knew more than he let on.

I was trying hard to delay Raj's paperwork but Mum kept on at me to get a move on with it. She wanted Raj to be here as soon as possible. I wanted to delay it so that Raj wouldn't be here for the birth, but the way things were going it seemed as though he would be here quicker than I expected.

The appointments at the midwife had now gone from four weeks to every two weeks. I felt that's all I ever did. They were much shorter in the sense she checked my urine, blood pressure, and weight and felt my abdomen to feel the position and growth of the baby. She listened to the baby's heartbeat which was quite strong. Sometimes she would let me listen to it to.

There was only one big fear which was stuck in the back of my head and that was giving birth. The thought about going into labour was killing me. I had read so many magazines and seen so many photos showing the pains of labour. How would I cope with all this? The day was coming closer and closer and I had to think what I wanted regarding pain relief to take me through the stages of labour. Mum talked as though it was simple as ABC, but to me it all seemed like a big nightmare. She said that she coped with just gas and air but I couldn't see myself coping on just gas and air. I wasn't brave like Mum. I was scared of even the slightest needle being poked inside of me. I thought of having the epidural but even that scared me after I found out that they stuck a needle into your spine and that you couldn't push when giving birth. I didn't feel like getting cut up by having a caesarean, as there was no way I was going to have a big scare on my stomach. I had already started to apply loads of cream on my stomach to stop me having any stretch marks after giving birth. I had heard many women talk about these horrible marks left on their stomachs after giving birth. I wanted my waist to look exactly how it was before I got pregnant. So far I had done everything possible to stop having those dreaded lines appearing across my stomach. Wasn't there an easy way out?

I stood by the mirror, which hung in my bedroom. I was looking humongous. My stomach stuck out like a water melon and all I wanted was to have the baby and get rid of the stomach, which made me look so big. I was quite conscious about how I dressed and looked; being pregnant wasn't anything to feel sexy about. As soon as I stopped getting into my size 10 jeans I hated it. I had to shop and get big clothes, which I wasn't very impressed about. Most of the maternity clothes I saw weren't trendy clothes that you saw teenagers in. I longed to get back into my own clothes but I just couldn't see that happening for a while. My face looked puffed up and my skin was so shiny that it glowed. Wearing makeup didn't really make me feel any better. I had also started putting clothes together for my big day. Although it was a while away I felt it was important in case I was rushed into hospital.

My feelings for the baby had changed considerably. I had mixed feelings maybe because I wasn't carrying Raj's baby but Sunny's. I never thought for a second that my feelings for the baby would change like this.

I hadn't started to shop for the baby either. I wasn't that eager to shop anyway. I just didn't feel bothered anymore. Mum was a bit sceptical about the whole idea of shopping early anyway. She said I should wait towards the end. I could see her point of view. I wasn't in a rush to buy any clothes, as I didn't know whether it was going to be a girl or a boy.

As I was upstairs, I decided to ring Raj. My feelings for Raj were growing more and more by the day. I never thought that anyone would replace Sunny but I was totally wrong. It took a while before I managed to get through on the phone to Raj.

'Hello can I speak to Raj please,' I said.

'Hello,' he said.

'Hi love, how are you?

'Hi Priya, how are you?'

'I'm fine, but missing you loads.'

'I've only just come home. I'm so happy, jaan; I've got good news today, I was just about to ring you to tell you the news.'

'What's the good news, tell me?'

I've got my visa and my plane ticket in my hand. I'm going to see you soon.'

As soon as I heard him say this I was shocked, I was lost for words, and instead of saying how fantastic that was... my face dropped and I was silent.

'Hi jaan, are you there?'

I spoke after a good few seconds pause.

'Yeah, that's umm great. So when are you coming over?'

'How does this Saturday sound?'

I was expecting him to say in a few weeks time not this Saturday!

'Saturday, don't you want to spend a bit of time with your family and sort out everything before you come?'

'You don't sound too happy that I'm coming.'

'No dear, I am, it's just that I wasn't expecting it to be this soon.'

'It's all sorted, don't worry jaan, I've taken care of everything, besides I've missed you so much that I can't wait to see you, these last few months without you have just been awful. Shall I give you my flight details?'

'Oh yes.'

I couldn't believe that Raj was going to be here on Saturday. After the phone call I went quickly downstairs to give Mum and Gran the good news. Of course, they were over the moon when I told them.

Although I was happy he was coming over, I was at the same time really scared, as I didn't want him here before the birth. I felt what I was doing was totally wrong but things had got so far that I couldn't stop it now. This was too much to take in now. I just had to carry on with this lie.

Mum had started to buy clothes for the baby. We bought mostly what the books told us that we would need like stretch suits, vests, shawl, blankets, cotton hat, socks, cardigan, nappies and other essential items. We hadn't brought the car seat, cot and other big items yet though.

CHAPTER 15

Priya's pregnant
(28-32 weeks)

The next few days our house turned into a madhouse. Mum had started shopping like crazy; she'd made the house look as though it had just been decorated. She hadn't left one area untouched. My bedroom was totally transformed after she had it painted and decorated. When Saturday arrived Mum was up quite early. As per usual she had cooked a meal for about twenty people. We left fairly early, so that we were at the airport in good time. I wasn't dressed to impress Raj; I mean how could I with my stomach hanging out and my face, which looked like I had swallowed a football.

When we arrived at the airport, Mum told me to sit down. I was glad that I had found somewhere to sit as my legs were killing me. It was a long and tiring wait. Maybe I should have listened to Mum, after all she did tell me to stop home but I couldn't disappoint Raj by not turning up on his first day in the UK. The plane had landed but there was no sign of Raj. Just as I was thinking of making some enquiries, Mum spotted him coming out. I was somewhat excited to see him. I got up and slowly walked towards where Mum was standing. I saw him smiling at me from a distance. He came out wearing a white shirt and a black jacket. I could tell that he had definitely lost some weight. His dark brown complexion just stood out. You could easily tell he was from India. When he came over he touched Mum and Gran's feet for their blessings. He saw me and gave me a hug. As we walked towards the car he talked about his journey on the plane.

His face said it all, he looked so happy. He spoke about how good the flight was and the food. He seemed over the moon that he had come to the UK; he was amazed by all the buildings and the developments here compared to India. He sat with me in the back of the car holding my hand. His eyes were glued to what he saw outside. By the time I got home I was extremely tired and I just needed to put my feet up. I showed Raj our bedroom and I took out some new clothes, which I had brought for him. I left him to freshen up while I went to ask Mum if she needed any help but Mum as usual sent me away. I didn't argue.

After lunch Aunt Neelam and my cousins came over to meet Raj. I felt it was rude to leave so I sat for a while and then left to rest. It was kind of strange being married, I mean in India it didn't feel that way but here it just seemed a bit weird. I just hadn't got to grips with the fact that we were now husband and wife. It felt strange. He was looking quite handsome in the jeans and t-shirt that I had brought for him, and although he had lost some weight, he was still muscular.

Raj started to unpack his suitcase. He was telling me

that he had brought me some beautiful outfits. He seemed a bit upset and I asked him what was wrong,

'Well I wasn't expecting you to be this big; I don't really think the Asian suits are going to fit you?'

'Oh, it doesn't matter, I'm not going to be big all my life, and it's just for a short while.'

'I guess so, anyway here take a look.'

He passed me a few suits which he had brought. I couldn't believe how beautiful they were. He had really good taste.

'I hope you like them, Priya?'

'They're so beautiful, Raj.'

I went over and gave him a big kiss on the lips. I could see a big smile appear on his face.

I was now questioning what love was, as what I had with Sunny didn't feel the same as what I now felt for Raj. I felt a different kind of love for Raj which I hadn't experienced with Sunny before. Deep down I didn't want to lose Raj. Just seeing him brought a smile to my face. I really admired his personality. He wasn't a serious type of guy but quite the opposite. It wasn't just me he got on well with but with anybody whether it was a child or someone elderly. If anyone came round he kept them quite amused. Raj wasn't concerned about how he looked or his macho image whereas Sunny was the opposite, his looks and his image meant the world to him. He had to show that he was something.

After I had been resting for a while Raj came upstairs. I was feeling a bit shy and nervous as he walked in. He came over to the bed as I was resting. He put his hand on my stomach as I lay on the bed. He spoke, looking at me,

'Our baby, isn't it, jaan?'

I looked at him and just didn't know what to say, I nodded.

'So how pregnant are you, Priya?'

I looked at him in dismay.

'Why do you keep asking me this?' I said.

'It's just that I was a bit shocked when your Mum first mentioned it on the phone, that you were pregnant. I didn't think you could get pregnant so easily.'

I looked at him; his face said it all. I started to feel scared and I responded quickly.

'Well I did, look is there something you want to say?' I replied.

'No, not really, just you know a bit shocked that you got pregnant when we hadn't really spent that much time together. I mean we only spent three nights together.'

'It's only been a few hours since you've come and already you're questioning me left, right and centre as though I've done something wrong.' I said defensively.

He stood looking at me and then spoke,

'Wouldn't you be shocked if you were in my position? I just thought we could spend some quality time together knowing one another before settling down and having kids. I just couldn't believe it when your mum told my mum.'

'So are you saying that this isn't your baby?'

'I didn't say that did I, you're going a bit too far saying that.'

'You started it!'

'Why are you so tensed then if it's our baby?'

I just shut up; there was a knock on the door,

'Priya, can I come in?' It was Mum.

'Yes, Mum'.

Is everything OK? She said standing at the door.

'Why wouldn't it be,' I replied.

'Are you coming down, Raj? Everyone's asking about you. Leave Priya here to rest while you come down for a bit. Will you be OK, Priya?' said Mum.

'Yes Mum, I'm fine, just need to rest a bit.'

Raj looked at me and gave me a small smile and then followed Mum downstairs. I was relieved when he left, my heart was racing really fast, and I was kind of panicking. I just didn't know how I was going to carry on lying to him. I could tell that he wasn't convinced that the baby was his. I knew lying to him wasn't the right thing to do, but it was too late. If I told him the truth now, then I would lose everything. I couldn't afford to gamble all that for one lie. I had to carry on lying and convince him that the baby was his.

In the back of my mind I felt that he knew the truth. Why else would he question me so much? On the phone he never once questioned me but now he was here he had started to fire questions which I felt I couldn't answer. As I rested in my room I started to scribble out my birth plan which I was told I should do. I jotted down where I was going to have the baby and what pain relief I was going to have. I decided that I would go just for gas and air and if the pain got worse I would have a pethidine injection.

My bag was already packed ready to take to the hospital. My ankles had swollen a bit; the midwife had told me that it was because my body had more water than usual. She said I should exercise my feet more. I was finding it very uncomfortable to lie down because my tummy was so big. I was scared to hurt the baby if anything. I put a few cushions behind me to make myself more comfortable but I knew that until long after the baby was born I wouldn't really get a goodnight sleep.

CHAPTER 16

Priya's pregnant
(32-36 weeks)

Since Raj had come it had been nearly two weeks. I could tell from the look on his face that he wasn't too happy. I didn't really know the reason for this, for all I knew it could be anything, he could be missing India and his parents, or he was getting bored staying at home couped up all day. His humour had suddenly disappeared and he had become all serious, which was very unlike him. He seemed to be annoyed and frustrated. Each time I questioned him, he wouldn't give me a straight answer. I didn't know if I was reading a bit too much into it but I thought it might be the fact that he was just tired of having no luck with finding a job. There wasn't much I could do either. Since he had come I couldn't really take him anywhere. Aunt Neelam's sons, Karim and Sahil had been really good and taken him out here and there but that was it.

As the weeks passed by I was feeling a lot more tired. The baby was growing bigger each week. I was eating so much, somehow my appetite seemed to be huge and all I wanted to do was eat. I felt hungry all the time. I was literally snacking all day which explained why I had suddenly grown so big. I looked like a big balloon which was going to pop any minute. I was also suffering from a lot of heartburn.

I was now more worried about myself, the last few days had been quite stressful as I was getting contraction pains. First I thought it was the real thing but it wasn't. I felt stupid when the doctors told me it was a false alarm. Raj was causing me more stress by acting like a stupid brat. I wasn't sure what was eating him up but something was really irritating him. He wouldn't discuss it with me either, which made matters worse. All we did was argue over his mood swings. Mum was telling me not to worry too much. Mum had also picked up that Raj wasn't very happy. He just kept to himself and said nothing. He spent a lot of time going over to Aunt Neelam's to be with Sahil and Karim. He had now joined college and was doing some sort of IT course.

I was now on the countdown, I only had a month to go before I gave birth. At this point I really wanted to get the baby out. My stomach was getting tighter and tighter and I kept having practise contraction pains but they were quite mild at this stage. I couldn't really imagine how the real contractions were going to feel.

I was going to see the midwife frequently. I had packed my bag properly for the big day. I wasn't sure how much I should pack but I had packed enough stuff so that I wouldn't run out, which came to something like two whole bags. Mum and Gran had mostly bought everything that the baby was going to need. I was lucky that Mum had paid for everything because on my own I don't think I would have been able to afford half the stuff. You can never imagine how much stuff one little baby needs, but it's a quite a lot. From the cot, the pram, the clothes, to the baby seat and nappies.

All day I just sat and rested; what else could I do? Aunt Neelam kept coming in to see how I was doing. Lately Raj had really started to go cold on me, I wasn't quite sure why but I really didn't have the energy to ask. There was no joy or laughter about the fact that he was going to be a father. I decided that once the baby was born I wouldn't lie to him about anything. All these lies so far had come from this baby I had decided to keep, I didn't want to lie to Raj anymore but I just had to keep up this lie for another few weeks and then I could stop once and for all.

Raj was spending a lot of his time out of the house with Karim, the two of them had bonded quite well together. I was quite happy about this because it gave Raj someone to spend time with. I wasn't any use at the moment; I couldn't really take him anywhere. I hadn't emailed Anita for a while either. After Raj had come I just hadn't had the time. I went upstairs to my room to email her. It was hard to sit at the computer with my stomach in the way. When I logged onto the computer I checked my emails. Anita had beaten me to it, I opened her message.

Hi Priya,

How are you? Has your husband come over from India, I am dying to see what he looks like. You'll have to send me a photo of him Priya. I've got some good news too. I've got a boyfriend, his name's Akash but I call him AK for short. I've sent you a photo of him, open the attachment and have a look. We met at a disco two weeks ago. He's really nice.

How are you keeping, is the baby OK? You haven't got long left to go have you? I told AK about you, he was shocked. Has Raj settled down with you or not? I wish we were all together Priya because we could have all done things together in a foursome. Anyway I'll catch up with u later, don't forget to send me a picture of your hubby, and say hello to aunty for me. Take care,

Phone me when you have the baby
Love Anita

I clicked on the attachment to see Anita's boyfriend's photo. The picture came up slowly. I was sort of shocked. It wasn't the type of guy Anita went for. He looked like a rich guy and wore very posh clothes. He was quite handsome. I don't know whether I felt a bit jealous, I knew that I shouldn't be but I just couldn't help the way I felt. Maybe because I was just sitting at home all day feeling sorry for myself I don't know. I started typing my response.

Hi Anita

I got yr mail. I saw AK's photo, you surely caught a whopper this time round. He's dead gorgeous, I'm jealous. Ha-ha! I've sent you Raj's photo, so take a look. Hope you like him.

I'm well, still waiting for the baby to come. I just want it over and done with now. I'm getting tired of just sitting all day. There's nothing I can really do. I feel like a couch potato. I've got swelling on both my ankles so I need to keep my feet up. Raj is settling down slowly but somehow he just doesn't look happy, and I think it's because he's missing his family. He doesn't say much so I can't really work out what's really bugging him. But I'm going to talk to him later. That's it really, nothing else happening.
Take care
Priya

After I logged off, I lay on my bed. I needed to talk to Raj and see why he was acting so cold. Since he had come to England I couldn't really do anything special with him. In India it was so different. He really made me enjoy the time I spent with him. I felt I hadn't done anything to show how much I really loved him. But what could I do, surely Raj could understand my dilemma? I didn't really have to spell it out to him did I? Mum and Gran had just come back from shopping. I could see Mum had brought loads of stuff for the baby. I felt Mum was more excited about the baby than I was. I just didn't feel excited anymore. In the beginning it was like nothing else mattered but since I had married Raj, I felt the tables had turned and the baby didn't really mean anything anymore. Maybe because I knew that it was Sunny's. I was scared. After the baby was born it would just remind me of Sunny. I felt terrible each time I thought like this. But there was no turning back now.

Today I had to go to the first antenatal class. I was feeling a bit on edge about going because of my age and also because I didn't know how Raj was going to be with me. I wasn't sure whether I should take him but there was no way I was going alone to these classes. I heard Raj walk in with Karim. They both came into the lounge holding this huge exercise machine.

'What's this?' I said looking at them both.

'It's for you to loose your weight after you've had the baby,' laughed Karim.

'Very funny.'

Karim said I could have his weights as he no longer needs them.'

'That's kind of you dear bro.'

'Well, I thought it'll give Raj something to do. I've got to go now so I'll leave you two love birds together.'

'See you later Karim.'

After Karim left I thought I'd mention the antenatal classes.

'Oh Raj, tonight it's my first antenatal class at the hospital, so will you come with me?'

'Why, what am I going to do there, isn't it for you women.'

'Well, all the husbands go with their wives, so I thought it'll be nice if you came with me too.'

'If you want, I'm just going to go upstairs and sort these weights out.'

I could tell that Raj didn't really want to come but he hadn't got much choice. I just had to wait and see how he would behave with me in the first antenatal class.

In the evening Mum drove Raj and me to the hospital. When we got there I saw so many other pregnant women standing outside the maternity building. I asked one of the ladies if they had come for the antenatal classes, she nodded and smiled. After a short while a lady came and greeted us all. She introduced herself and took us all inside. I sat down next to Raj. The lady talked for a long while about why we were there and what she was going to talk about. She got us to do some breathing and relaxation exercises. I felt really uncomfortable; it wasn't something you normally do. I could tell Raj wasn't enjoying the class at all. He was just sitting and not participating. I was glad when it had finished. I felt out of place; we were the youngest couple there and everyone else just looked liked they knew what they were doing. Mum had come to pick us up, all the way home Raj hardly said a word to me about how he felt. When I got home I was in tears. I felt like just telling Raj the whole truth. I was sick of all this lying. He saw me crying but said nothing but left me to cry, which I couldn't really understand.

The next few weeks went fairly quickly. Raj and me were getting on better than before. He had started talking all of a sudden, which made me feel so much better. I had asked him why he was cold with me but all he said was I will tell you when the time's right. I couldn't make out what he meant by that, I was worried that he still doubted me about the baby.

Becky phoned me when the results of the A levels were out. She was over the moon as she had got very good grades. She told me that Sunny had just about scraped through, and that Rina had done exceptionally well. She asked me how I was doing. I told her I was OK, I mean what more could I say, I was quite big now and all I wanted was to have the baby. I wanted to get on with life again instead of sitting and resting all the time, which was something I wasn't used to doing.

I was quite upset for a few days. I too had dreamt about going to uni and doing a teaching degree, if anything I could have made it if I hadn't decided to keep the baby. I felt quite tired and although I tried to keep myself active by going for short walks and that I couldn't get one worry out of my head and that was how Raj was going to react if he ever found out that he wasn't the father of the baby. Each day I sat down and jotted something in my pregnancy diary, which the midwife had given me. I had written quite a bit inside it about how I was coping with my daily aches and pains to how I was feeling.

CHAPTER 17

Priya's pregnant
39 weeks onwards

I was now 39 weeks pregnant. I had another appointment with the midwife. I couldn't believe that any week now I was going to give birth. I was pretty scared. The thought of labour was scaring the living daylights out of me. It was the pain I was worried about more than anything else.

Mum dropped us off at the Health Care Centre. There were so many people at the clinic when we arrived. We didn't have to wait too long before we were called in. Each time I visited the midwife she had a student with her. Although my blood pressure and urine was checked by the midwife, my abdomen was felt by the student. The midwife would stand behind her as she checked me. She did ask me if I was happy for a student to check me, and of course I never refused, I mean it was the only way for them to learn the job I presume. This time when I went the midwife was alone without any student. So today she examined my abdomen. I didn't really think anything was going to be wrong as everything was going OK. She kept feeling my stomach and I was feeling a bit anxious about this. As she examined me she told me that the baby had turned and it looked like that it was in a breech position. I was really worried as to what would happen now. On the last visit I was told that the baby was moving down and everything was fine and I had nothing to worry about. I questioned the midwife about this,

'I thought you said the baby was moving down last time I came.'

'Well it may have been but since then it has turned around.'

'So what happens now?' I said looking really worried.

'You will have to go to the hospital and see if they can either turn the baby around and if not then you may have to have a caesarean. Your blood pressure is still high and there's a good chance they will have to perform a caesarean rather than you having a natural birth.'

Raj was sitting looking really worried by what the midwife was saying. All of a sudden she started to mention that I was 39 weeks pregnant and that I needed to go to the hospital tomorrow for a scan to double check that it was in breech position. I phoned Mum and she came to pick us up from the Health Care Centre. I told Mum in the car what the midwife had said. Mum told me not to worry. Raj didn't say a single word in the car. When I got home he told me to come upstairs in the bedroom, he said he wanted to talk to me.

As I was going up the stairs I was trying to work out what Raj wanted to talk to me about. I went inside the room; Raj was sitting on the bed. I went over and sat next to him.

'How can you be 39 weeks pregnant?'

I looked at him and just didn't know what to say.

'This isn't my baby, is it?'

I turned totally white. I couldn't get any words out to say anything.

'I just knew it, you know all this time I've been cold towards you is because I never believed that this was my baby, I mean how can it be? Nothing adds up; when I saw you at the airport I just couldn't believe how big you looked. We do have pregnant women in India too you know, did you really think you could fool me? Why lie about this? Did you really think I was that stupid?'

My heart was racing and I felt unwell. All of a sudden he put his hand on my stomach.

'Swear by this baby, that this baby is mine.'

All of a sudden I could feel my head swaying and suddenly everything just went black.

When I woke up again I was in hospital. I could see Mum standing by my side; there was no sign of Raj. I had tears rolling down the side of my cheeks. I wondered if Raj had told Mum about me. I stayed quiet. Mum asked how I was feeling. She filled me in on what had happened.

'Don't worry, you collapsed and we had to call the ambulance. They're going to take you to have a caesarean. You've got nothing to worry about. Just relax.'

I lay there saying nothing.

Later when I woke up I could see the baby by my side. Mum asked how I was feeling. She held the baby towards me.

'Look it's a boy, Priya.

I smiled.

I looked at Mum and then the baby, which she held in her arms. When Mum handed me the baby I couldn't believe that he was mine. He was so small and so light. He lay in my arms peacefully and I felt a rush of pride to be holding my son. All these months of keeping him inside me had paid off. He was so adorable; I just couldn't explain that feeling of love that I had inside. He looked just like Sunny; in fact he was a copy of him. But then I felt saddened by this. I thought of Raj and what had happened just before I had collapsed. I looked around; there was no sign of Raj still.

Where's Raj, Mum?'

Mum looked at me,

'Don't worry he'll come soon, he's probably with Karim and Sahil.'

The midwife came in later to show me how to breastfeed but it seemed like a mammoth task in itself. The baby just wouldn't latch on. After a few attempts though I had picked it up.

Tears started to fall from my eyes as I thought about the consequences I would have to face after the truth finally came out in the open. Raj had already found out the truth, soon Mum and Aunt Neelam and everyone else would find out too.

Mum came over,

'What is it Priya why are you crying?'

'I don't know, Mum, I just don't know.'

She took the baby off me and put him in the cot next to me. I lay back down gently; my stomach was feeling really sore, as the drugs had started to wear off.

Later that day Aunt Neelam arrived with Gran, followed by Sahil and Karim. There was still no sign of Raj. After a few hours Mum and Gran decided to go home for a bit. Aunt Neelam stayed behind and so did Karim; they came over to the bed.

'Priya we need to talk.'

I looked at them; there was a serious look on their faces that I hadn't seen before.

'What is it? I asked.

'It's about Raj.'

'Is he OK?'

'He's fine, don't worry, he's told us about the baby, that it's not his.'

I started to cry.

'Priya, is Raj telling the truth, I need to know?' asked Aunt Neelam.

'Yes it's true, he's not the father.'

'So who is then?'

'Sunny, the guy I was seeing at college.'

Karim and Aunt Neelam didn't look very impressed with me, they both sighed,

'How did Raj find out?'

'He mentioned something about your pregnancy diary.'

'But I always hid it so that he wouldn't find it.'

'Priya, did you really think you would get away with lying to him about something so big? He said that he had doubts on you ever since you told him on the phone that you were pregnant. He said that if he started to accuse you too early on then you might not have filed the paperwork. He needed to get proof that he wasn't the father. He also found other stuff too.'

'Like what?'

'Your scan photos with the dates on them when you had them done. He worked out that you were pregnant before you went to India. Why did you do that, Priya?'

There were more tears, as I just didn't have an answer to give him.

'I loved Sunny, and at that time when I found out I was pregnant I just couldn't kill an innocent baby. It was Uncle Mahesh and Mum who told me to get married. Mum said she was all alone and that, so I felt helpless. I didn't want to marry Raj but Raj liked me and he wouldn't take no for an answer. I did try and tell him I had a past but he wasn't that bothered about my past. Everything's so messed up now and it's all my fault.'

'Where is he? Karim, tell me.'

'He's staying at my mate's house.'

'What does he want to do?'

'He's given me this letter to give you.'

Karim pulled out a letter from his jacket and handed it to me. I quickly opened it,

Priya

I really thought you were the right girl for me. How wrong of me to even think like that. I can't stay with

you anymore. I didn't want to start throwing accusations at you when I hadn't any proof, but now the truth is out.

I hate you Priya, how could you betray me so badly. What did I ever do to you? All I did was fall in love with you. Did you really think you could get away with it by telling me that I was the father of the baby? So, you were pregnant before we met, how sick!

I haven't told your Mum about this, I thought I let you do the talking since you're so good at it. Even if I told them, do you think they would believe me? I no longer want to stay with you; I can't live with a liar and a cheat! How can I live with you knowing that the baby is someone else's? Do whatever you have to do, don't even bother looking for me or trying to explain your reasons because I'm not interested, you hear.

A word of advice, don't ever break anyone else's heart, the way you broke mine.
Raj

Tears fell as I read his angry words.

'What's he written?' asked Aunt Neelam.

'Just leave me alone,' I sobbed. Aunt Neelam and Karim walked out, leaving me alone. What had I done? I felt so ashamed of myself. I felt greedy and selfish. I hadn't thought about the consequences of what would happen the day Raj found out about the baby. All I was interested in was myself. I knew I would have to pay the price for this. How would I make Raj understand? Soon Mum would be asking me questions about Raj too, what would I say to her? I cried and cried but the truth that Raj had left me would not leave my head. As I cried Mum walked in.

'What happened, Priya why are you crying?'

What could I say, I just cried and cried. I would have to tell her, no matter what. I handed her Raj's letter. Mum stood up and started to read the letter by the window. As she read the letter tears fell from her eyes. She then looked at me in disgrace,

'You didn't have the abortion, did you?'

I shook my head.

'I'm so sorry Mum, I'm really, really sorry.'

She came towards me and slapped me across my face.

'I should have done this a long time ago,' she said angrily and she walked out.

I was all alone, the baby and me. There was no Sunny or Raj. How was I going to bring up this baby without anyone's help or support? God had given me exactly what I deserved. I stayed at the hospital for a few days but Mum never came to see me after that. I knew that she was really mad with me. The only people who came to visit were Aunt Neelam and her two sons. Aunt Neelam suggested that I give the baby up for adoption. She said that after speaking to my Mum she didn't think that she would help me bring up my baby. She had made it quite clear she didn't want anything to do with this baby. I just didn't know what to do? This baby meant the world to me, how could I give up my own flesh and blood? At the same time, how was I going to look after it? There was no-one to help me. Aunt Neelam had also made it clear that if she helped then her relationship with Mum would break and she couldn't do that.

The doctors were keeping me in as my blood pressure was still quite high. I had started to take tablets for it and had stopped breastfeeding as I wasn't producing enough milk to feed the baby. I was feeling very low inside. Aunt Neelam was pushing me to feed the baby. I felt like the world had ended for me. I had lost Raj who I really loved and I had a baby, which my family had rejected. Karim tried his best to cheer me up but I just couldn't pull myself together. I felt alone and depressed. I decided it was time I spoke to Social Services, maybe they could help. That night I thought whether I should write to Raj. I had to explain my reasons for what I had done. Karim suggested that it was the right thing to do. He said he would try his best to bring him around. Aunt Neelan and Karim left me for a while. The nurse came in telling me that there was a call for me, and asked if I wanted to take it. It was Anita.

'Hello.'

'It's me, Anita.'

I started crying.

'Hey, why are you crying?-I phoned your house and your Mum told me that you had had the baby and that. Your Mum didn't say too much. Has something happened Priya, even your Mum seemed very upset when I spoke to her?'

'Did she tell you?'

'No, she said nothing. Anyway how are you?'

'I'm OK, I think.'

'I heard you had a boy, I bet he's cute. You must be real proud.'

'I don't know, Anita.'

'Hey Priya, what's wrong, why are you saying that?'

'I've lost everything, Mum no longer comes to see me, Raj has found out he isn't the father of the baby. What am I going to do?'

'Look, it will all get sorted, give it time.'

'No, not this time Anita, Raj wrote me a letter saying he doesn't want to know me after all this.'

'He doesn't really mean it, he's angry right now; you have to give it time. You have to explain to Raj why you did what you did Priya. At the moment he thinks you've done all this for yourself; you have to tell him how you felt and why you did what you did. Write him a letter Priya and tell him. You haven't got anything to lose believe me. Tell him how much he means to you. Tell him that you love him.'

'There's no point Anita, I've got what I deserved. What's the point, there's no way he's going to listen to me now. I don't know whether I should talk to a Social Worker and tell them how I'm feeling.'

'Don't tell them just yet, first write to Raj and see how he reacts. Just remember Priya, if he loves you then he'll come back. Priya, do it for me at least, all I'm asking is for you to write one last letter to him, please Priya.'

'OK, I'll do it.'

'Thanks, that's more like the Priya I know. Don't give up. I know life isn't easy for you right now, but I'm still here for you. I might be far away but I'm still here to be your friend.'

'Thanks Anita, I'm so glad you phoned. I really felt like giving up.'

'Remember Priya never give up without a fight. Write it now; don't wait till tomorrow you hear. I'll phone again soon, I've got to go.'

I didn't waste any time and quickly put pen to paper,

Dear Raj

I know right now that I am the last person you want to speak to. I never meant to hurt you. I didn't think things would turn out like this. I am so sorry, I am prepared to do anything you say to bring you back to me. I want you to give me one last chance, that's all I'm asking for. I know I am not worthy for what I have done but please can you find it in your heart to forgive me. I am already paying the price for what I have done.

I will not deny the truth, yes, I did have a boyfriend and yes I was pregnant and it was his baby and not yours. He wanted me to get rid of the baby but I couldn't, Raj, how could I kill an innocent life that was growing inside me and that I was responsible for?

When I came to India I had no idea that Mum wanted me to get married. I only came thinking that I was going to attend Sneha's wedding. I had no intentions on marriage and I told you that. I tried explaining to you that I had a past but you didn't seem very interested about it. Maybe if you did, then I would have told you. But it's my fault for keeping it a secret from you. I realise now what I have done was wrong, and I need you to forgive me otherwise I don't think I could live anymore. I hate myself Raj, I am very sorry. I love you very, very much and I need you.

Please, please come back.

Yrs Priya

As I sat in bed, Karim walked into the room, behind him stood Raj. My jaw dropped as I saw his face after such a long time. I had really missed him. I couldn't believe he was standing there.

'I'll leave you two here to talk, I'll be back later.'
Karim walked out leaving Raj and me in the room together. My eyes had already started to fill up again. I was so happy to see him. He came over; he looked at the baby and said nothing.

'I'm really, really sorry Raj,' I said, holding his hand as he stood by the bed.

'Sorry for what, Priya? Sorry that you lied to me, sorry that the baby's not ours, sorry for what?'

I didn't know what to say, I just cried.

'I loved you Priya, I loved you so much, that there wasn't a single minute when you weren't in my mind. The only reason I am standing here right now is because I'm not a guy who runs when the going gets tough. You forget I was born in India and in India we don't treat anyone in a horrible manner like the way you have treated me. You are lucky that I'm not from here otherwise I would have walked straight out. I don't deserve someone like you.'

'You're right, you shouldn't be with someone like me, and if you leave me then I can't blame you because it's all my fault. But I didn't fake our love. I love you so much, Raj. The time I spent with you in India made me realise what a nice guy you are. I never felt this way about anyone. You mean so much to me, but how can I make you believe that? The last few days while I have been sitting here in bed I have been thinking about the wrong I have done, I never meant to hurt you. I didn't come to India to marry anyone but Mum wanted me to get married. I tried telling you that I had a past but you didn't show any interest in that.'

'You know people here are so different to people in India. I thought everyone here was so caring like back home but that's not true at all. If anything people here are selfish, they only think about themselves and they lie so much that it doesn't even affect them. You might not have taken the marriage vows seriously but I did. Priya, you're supposed to be my wife, is this how you women treat men? Is this what happens when you marry an Indian guy? You know since I found out, I haven't slept. I have left my own country to be with you, not only that, I've left my parents, everything to be with you and this is how you repay me. I have only come here today because Karim told me how upset you had been. He told me that you had told your mum too. Although you could do all this to me, I couldn't do that to you. I'm giving you a second chance.'

I looked up at him hopefully.

'I promise you Raj, you will not have a chance to complain. The three of us...'

'What do you mean the three of us? You've got to choose between me and the baby.'

'What do you mean?'

'You will have to choose either the baby or me. One has to go. If you want the baby then you cannot have me, and if you choose me then you have to give the baby away.'

I looked at him.

'You've caused me so much pain, Priya; you can't expect me to bring up someone else's baby. I can't ever be the father of your lover's baby. You have to choose. You can have some time to think about it.'

I was shocked at the ultimatum Raj had given me. Although Sunny was the father of the baby, I was the mother of the baby too. How could I leave an innocent baby to the care of someone else? Up to now the baby had meant everything to me. What kind of mother would I be if I gave him up? How could I abandon him when his life had just begun? Sunny was out of the picture altogether and if I lost Raj then how could I support a baby on my own? There was no way mum was going to help me. I looked at the baby lying in the cot. I never thought that it would come to me choosing between my husband and my baby. Although I deeply loved Raj I just couldn't give up my baby. I had to face the consequences of my actions, even if that meant I would have to raise him on my own. I had to do it.

'I don't want to lose you Raj; I love you very very much, but I cannot give up my baby.' I held his hand tightly as I spoke.

A tear fell from his eye. This was the first time I had seen him cry. He let go of my hand and started heading towards the door of my room.

'Raj please understand what I'm going through. Why are you separating me from my baby? You know that for any mother it's not easy to give up a child that has been carried inside her for nine months.'

He turned around and said sadly,

'Well there's no way I can bring up someone else's baby.'

'Listen to me Raj… please Raj!'

Next minute he was gone. I sat crying. It was all over between us.

CHAPTER 19

I tried very hard to bring up my baby on my own but I struggled. I became depressed and my family had cut their ties with me altogether. Aunt Neelam and my cousin brothers had also lost contact with me. I was given a council house to live in but the stress and pressure had really got to me.

Then one day I made the decision to give my baby up for adoption. I knew that I couldn't give him any kind of happy life. I felt it was the only option left open to me. It was the hardest and most difficult thing I have ever done but I had very little choice.

Two years on and I still think about my baby. One day I will find out who he's staying with and what he's doing. I know he's never going to forgive me for giving him up but what choice did I have? Before I gave him up for adoption I had named him Akash, meaning '*sky*'. After I gave him up I moved to my own apartment in a different town subsequent to getting a part-time job at a nearby store. I really had learned the hard way.

Seventeen isn't an age when you've really grown up and can take on the responsibility of a baby and marriage, to a certain extent you're still mastering all the skills in life that needs to be learnt. Responsibility too early on isn't good because you haven't built the foundation to walk on. It's like a wall without cement, without the cement it's bound to collapse. I forgot that being a teenager is really supposed to be the best time of your life; I just wanted to grow up too early and take on responsibility that I couldn't really handle. I had let my whole family down, I felt disgusted with myself. I had left a black mark on my name for what I had done. Although I wasn't very religious or cultural I felt I had done wrong by having sex before marriage, which we Hindus believe is wrong and is seen as a sin.

When I gave birth I didn't really feel like I was a mother, possibly because I was just a kid myself. I know if Grandad were here today he would be very disappointed with me. I hadn't been fair on Mum at all, if anything I should be looking after her but all I caused her was pain and grief. She didn't deserve this, especially after Dad left. I keep questioning myself why I did it? Only one answer comes into my head each time and it was because I wanted love from my family. I thought when I met Sunny, I had found what was missing but really I used Sunny as a shield—someone to talk to about my problems. I missed having a dad and I too wanted to enjoy life with both parents, not one. I know my Dad's never going to come back and maybe I should accept this but I felt all these years I hadn't really accepted this. I don't know what dangerous game I was playing, but the game was now over. I felt I wanted to break free from all the things Mum didn't want me to do like meet my own guy, stay out until late and that but I now understand that these restrictions were for my own benefit really. Once a girl becomes pregnant like I did it's difficult for her to be accepted in the community and by her family.

I now needed to rectify my mistakes and to pray to God that he would help me achieve my goal, and that was to first re-do my A levels and then go to university and become an Art teacher, which was my goal in the first place. I now had to go two steps back when all my mates had now reached their goal. Although I had realised my mistakes I needed counselling, as I felt so depressed inside myself. I wasn't going to go to counselling but Anita persuaded me that it wasn't something I should feel ashamed of doing. She was right; I thought that all these years I didn't take anyone's advice as I thought that I knew it all but now I have started to listen to other people's advice more. Sometimes it's important to take time to listen instead of just leaping ahead like I had done.

I was entangled in a web of lies, which left me nowhere really. I had a baby at the wrong time; I left college without any A levels. All my other mates have got something to look forward to but what did I have to show for it? I'd locked all the doors to success. From my experience I've learnt that having fun isn't about getting pregnant or doing something which you're going to regret but staying within your limits; crossing your limits and taking the wrong steps before hand isn't going to take you anywhere.

In the past when Mum always sounded as if she was giving me lectures about what a girl should and shouldn't do, I felt that she was talking about how things used to be, but now I understand she was right in what she said. I can also now understand why Rina didn't push her limits, it's because her parents brought her up in a way that meant that she would follow the right path.

Trust is a big word, once it's lost it's very hard to get back. Raj taught me a lot and even though we're not together anymore I don't blame him one bit because it was all due to my lies that things didn't work out. If I hadn't become pregnant then I could still be living happily with Raj today. He deserves someone much better than me and I hope that he finds her too. As for me, I went back to square one, that is I returned to college to finish my education and work towards the career and life that I had always dreamed of.

Glossary of Asian Words

Ek, do, tin	–	One, two, three
Beti	–	Daughter
B.G	–	British Girl
B.A.G	–	British Asian Girl
Daal	–	Curry
Dandi	–	Village name
Halva	–	Asian sweet
Jaan	–	Darling
Mangal Sutra	–	A necklace which a husband gives to his wife on their wedding day
Masala Dosa	–	An Indian vegetarian dish
Meri Jaan	–	My Love
Pithi	–	Yellow paste applied on the body
Priya Ki Kahani	–	Priya's story
Sundari	–	Beautiful
Tilak	–	A red spot marked on the forehead